SECRETS IN THE DEEP BLUE SEA

JEULIA HESSE

DEEP CREEK PUBLISHERS

Copyright © 2023 by Jeulia Hesse

All rights reserved. No part of this publication may be reproduced, stored or transmitted in any form or by any means, electronic, mechanical, photocopying, recording, scanning or otherwise without written permission from the publisher. It is illegal to copy this book, post it to a website, or distribute it by any other means without permission. This novel is entirely a work of fiction. The names, characters and incidents portrayed in it are the work of the author's imagination. Any resemblance to actual persons, living or dead, events or localities is entirely coincidental.

Cover copy created by BlurbWriter.com

ALSO BY JEULIA HESSE

The Stone House Inn Series

- *Deadly Inheritance*

- *Killer Recipe*

- *Soul Sentinel*

The Deep Blue Sea Series

- *Secrets in the Deep Blue Sea*

- *Sins in the Deep Blue Sea*

- *Ghosts from the Deep Blue Sea* (coming Fall 2023)

CONTENTS

PROLOGUE

The sharp rising panic in her mother's voice drew her from the teenage retreat of her bedroom. She perched on the hard, narrow staircase leading to the kitchen, as the sound of her mother's voice carried through the stairwell. She kept out of her mother's line of sight, watching and listening intently to determine what was going on. The acrid smell of the smoke from her cigarette seeped up to Lizzie's hiding place, burning her eyes. Her mother never smoked in the house.

Something was wrong.

Her heavily accented voice peppered questions to the person on the other end of the phone, not giving a moment for an answer. The plastic on the old receiver of the kitchen wall phone creaked as she clutched it. From her mother's interrogations, it was obvious she was conversing with Cami's best friend, Lydia, grilling her to tell her of her sister's whereabouts.

Lizzie sighed heavily. Cami getting into trouble was nothing new. Not being where she was supposed to be, or with who she was supposed to be with, was kind of her thing. Her disappearances were routinely temporary, showing up after curfew or when she thought her mother had worried enough.

Something was different today. Lizzie remained rooted to the stairs, her mother's behavior making her curious to find out more. This was not her usual anger and frustration with the disobedience of her eldest child. She was worried, nearly panicked. Freaking out was not in her mother's usual limited range of emotions. There was anger, something she excelled at, with a dramatic flair and passion Lizzie had always assumed came from her Cuban heritage, shouting in Spanish whenever she was angry. The rest of her emotional palette ranged from stoic melancholy to downright unapproachable.

Over the past few hours, despite her earlier teenage self-absorption, Lizzie was aware of her mother's conversations while she talked on the old landline phone on the wall in the kitchen, just beneath her bedroom. The sound of the receiver slamming down, vibrating through the air and cutting through Lizzie's concentration on her book, and her never ending text conversations with her cousin and best friend, Marcus. As the afternoon went on, her mother's voice on the phone became more and more frantic.

From what Lizzie could piece together. Cami's boss had called later this morning, asking if her older sister was coming to work. Both Lizzie and her mother had dropped her off earlier that morning at the local Fort Zachary Taylor beach, where she was a lifeguard. Cami was the first person to greet young swimmers in the morning when they arrived for their lessons. It was summer break, and the locals were eager to get their young ones engaged in some kind of activity. Cami, along with another lifeguard, would oversee the little kids splashing on the beach, learning to float and put their faces in the water.

Unfortunately, Cami had a poor reputation, having had a few troubled years of falling into the wrong crowd around Key West. It was easy enough to do. Growing up smack dab in the middle of a tourist destination, there was plenty to get into trouble with. Their mother's family home was a few doors down from Hemmingway's. Her family was a part of the past aristocracy of the area, more infamous than celebrated. The family home just steps away from the touristy Duval Street, where a local could infiltrate the party scene.

Cami had reformed some at her parents' urging to consider her future. Her chances of getting into a good college quickly diminishing the less time she spent at school. Eventually she'd relented, agreeing to the rules they laid down. Her parents were determined to keep her out of trouble, so they encouraged her to take this job, to stop her from seeking any idle opportunities.

Her current boyfriend was a fisherman, and although their parents tolerated him, Lizzie didn't like him. He was much older in his early 20s. Cami was four years older than Lizzie's fourteen. Neither one of them was happy with her frequent attempts to join them when hanging out around the island. Clearly they thought her the pain in the butt younger sister and made clear they didn't want her around.

She was always an early riser, even on her school breaks, and had been in the back seat when they drove Cami to the beach this morning. Riding along was something to do and offered a chance to talk with her mother alone if Soledad was in the mood. She had no idea if Cami had any other plans for the day other than work. She wouldn't have shared them with her, anyway.

As much as Lizzie desired to be close with Cami, she rarely wanted anything to do with her. It didn't deter her; it seemed she'd had been trying her whole life. She adored and admired her older sibling and wanted to be just like her, except for the getting into trouble parts. Cami was beautiful and popular; all the things Lizzie wasn't. Her cheeks flared with acne outbreaks, and she was chubby and asthmatic; she was hideous and could barely stand herself. Really, she couldn't blame Cami for putting her off.

They had been arguing as mothers and daughters do on the short ride out to the beach.. Mother had lectured Cami about her obligations to meet in her job as a lifeguard, and Cami was furious when their mother set a 10 o'clock curfew for her and her boyfriend. She had left in a huff, her face flushed with anger as she slammed the car door shut and strode away.

Cami had always not responded well to limitations in her social life. Likely, this time was no different. But then why was Mother so panicked?

Their parents had aspirations for their daughter to attend college and do something more with her life than her mother had accomplished. Older than most other mothers among Lizzie's friends, she had a career of being a jazz singer in the local bars and clubs. Soledad had enjoyed some fame years ago, having recorded albums circulated across the world. Including being featured in several magazine stories, one in the National Geographic as part of the story on the Wislers, a local treasure hunting family. They'd found treasure in a shipwreck and the magazine connected her mother to the owner, getting her a small part in the overall story on Key West. She had something against them the Wisler's, but Lizzie didn't know her reasons. They were to be avoided. Her mother tolerated her relationship with Marcus's friend Daniel, but didn't welcome him into their home. This left the trio to hang out unsupervised at Marcus's house, his parents otherwise occupied with their busy social lives, leaving servants to oversee their children.

As one of the first families to settle on the island, Lizzie's mother's family boasted a rich and storied history. Her mother's family members were acquainted with many high-profile and wealthy individuals. Lizzie was aware her family was well off, but they were far from wealthy compared to others in the area. Her mother's brother, cousin Marcus's father, was among one of the ultra-wealthy. Lizzie's father, an island outsider, referred to them as "Cuban pirates". This was one secret they would share and smile about when they were out of her mother's hearing. She smiled fondly at the thought of her dad's gentle ribbing of her mother's family. She'd always thought them such an unlikely couple.

The phone conversations continued with Lizzie trying to piece the one-sided conversations together. From what she could gather, her sister had apparently taken her position on the lifeguard stand. Her towels and sandals were there from early this morning. But she was nowhere to be found. She had shown up to work, evidently intending to stay, but had left her post. There was an opened first aid kit on the bottom step of the chair, as though she had helped someone or herself to tend to an injury.

The first swimmers had no recollection of seeing her at the beach. Her co-lifeguard had been angry that Cami had not shown up for work, but he'd made nothing more of it than the old irresponsible Cami had just not shown up, leaving him to do the lessons himself and deal with the frantic, urgent mothers that were dropping off and picking up their children. Not only that, he'd have to keep an eye out for the other swimmers that morning. It wasn't until the park manager made the morning rounds that they realized something was very wrong.

Her mother continued to make another series of calls, which further raised Lizzie's alarm. Her mouth had gone dry, and an unease settled in her stomach as she wondered what Cami was up to now and if she realized the anguish it caused. The situation became real when her father arrived home early from work.

Lizzie's father, a surgeon who traveled back and forth to Boston as a professor at Harvard Medical School, had a local office on the island. He rarely ever came home before 6 PM and was more likely to arrive later in the evening if the hospital needed his services for emergencies. His presence validated her mother's worry was more than her usual response to Cami's antics. Lizzie could hear their low voices and her anxiety rose as her father worked to gain a handle on the situation through her mother's panic. He was the calm in the ever-swirling storm of her mother and sister's interactions. Lizzie and her father had a close relationship; she realized long ago that she was more like him than either her mother or her half-sister. He was her rock, the source of sanity in the craziness of teenage mothers and daughters.

"Do you feel we should involve the police?" her father asked, his voice both calm and urgent, a miracle borne of years practicing in serious medical situations.

Lizzie's mother shook her head, hesitantly. "Do you think James? Do you think we should? This isn't quite like her. No one has seen her since this morning. Not even her boyfriend."

James sighed deeply, raking his hand through his graying dark hair. Lizzie knew he really disliked her older sister's friends and worked hard to accept them. Even though Cami was not his child, he had taken or tried to take responsibility for her and give her a guiding push. Cami had rebelled against him.

"Why don't you call the police? At least we'll have a report and with them. I'll go to the pier to check on her boyfriend. See if he knows anything."

Soledad reached up and grabbed his hand as he stood, readying himself to leave. "James, I just know something is wrong. I can *feel* it."

They momentarily looked into each other's eyes; her mother's full of tears. "Be careful," she said as he turned to leave. The warning made Lizzie wonder why it was offered. Was there a reason for caution with Cami's boyfriend?

He left after kissing her cheek. Tears poured freely down her face as her mother thought she was alone. Soledad took several deep breaths to solidify herself and dialed the number to the local sheriff's office.

Lizzie heard bits and pieces of her conversation on the phone as she strained to hear. Her mother was told by the police that they would come by the house. Lizzie slipped down the stairs, worry churning in her belly, and wrapped her arms around her mother's waist. Soledad uncharacteristically returned the embrace, her ample arms fiercely clasping her younger daughter to her.

"Hija?" she asked, pulling back and grabbing Lizzie's face in her hands. "Do you know where your sister is?"

Her dark brown, tearful eyes bored into her own. She shook her head, her eyes welling, influenced by her mother's panic.

She wished she knew. Cami should have shared her plans and thoughts with her. But she wasn't that kind of sister.

Her mother knew this about her daughters' relationship and didn't press further. "Don't go anywhere today. Stay home, yes?" she both asked and demanded, retreating to the cadence of her native Spanish language.

Soledad pushed her away, shushing her from the kitchen. "See if Marcus has an idea? He knows as much of what happens on this island as anyone."

Lizzie happily sought refuge in her bedroom, eager to text Marcus and her closest friends and see if she could help by finding out the latest gossip and if there had been mention of her sister. Cami's reputation was often the topic of conversation, sparking curiosity and speculation. All of them agreed to check with people they knew to see if they had seen Cami today. Marcus was nothing more than helpful and kind, as he had been her entire life. In some ways, she was grateful for their relationship. In others, she wished it was like that with Cami, instead of with her male cousin.

While she waited for any word, Lizzie searched social media to see if there was any information to go by. Her anxiety rising as she waited, powerless to do anything more.

The text outreach found no additional details about Cami. No one had seen her today. Everyone agreed to reach out if they came across any news. Marcus offered to come to the house, but she turned him down, not wanting to be distracted from any new developments. Her gut kept telling her that something was off.

Sometime later, Lizzie overheard the adults in the kitchen talking with the sheriff. Her father re-counted his visit with Cami's boyfriend at the pier. He'd been adamant he hadn't heard from her. He reported they'd broken up a few days ago, and he hadn't seen her since. In fact, he had been in port all this time for boat repairs. The police could follow up on his story and ensure that he had indeed not left port to go out on the ocean to fish, potentially taking her sister with him. The news of the breakup was a revelation. Neither parent had heard of it.

Unfortunately, they were not unfamiliar with having the police sitting at the kitchen table talking about her sister and the trouble she had gotten in. Over time, there had been a stolen car, a rental, taken for a joyride. Drugs found with her or one of her boyfriends or underage drinking in the park. The police would always bring her home, their parents would continually thank them and, of course, try to discipline her sister.

Lizzie could tell that this time the stress level in the kitchen was very different, and her concern grew. Her father had apparently pressed the police to take her mother's concern seriously, that this was more than a troubled teenager's temporary run off. Lizzie gathered the police were already searching the beach. However, because so much time had elapsed from the time Cami had initially gone missing to now, they were not hopeful of finding a clue to her whereabouts.

After they had dropped Cami off at the beach, to the time the police were called, had been several hours, almost the entire beach day. Although she'd initially gone there, the police believed, but then something had occurred to pull her away. They hypothesized maybe she helped someone who'd been injured because of the opened first aid kit. No one had seen her since. The time lapse from when she disappeared to when someone realized something wasn't right had been pretty substantial. Beach goers and other lifeguards had trampled the scene all day. The activity compromising any evidence that might be on the beach.

Lizzie's mind raced as her heart rate rose. *Did the police really think something was wrong?* That someone may have *taken* her? The mention of 'scene' was making her nauseous. Had something terrible happened?

Heart racing, she retreated to her room and fumbled to dial Marcus's cell phone number. He immediately picked up. In hushed and frantic tones, Lizzie relayed what she'd overheard. "It sounds... it sounds serious," she sobbed into her pink sparkly iPhone.

"The police are at the beach? Can you get away?" he asked, ever her co-conspirator. "Slip out, Lizzie. Take your bike. I'll meet you there. Let's check it out."

Her parent's attention otherwise diverted with the police in the kitchen. Lizzie crept out the front door and pedaled to the beach. It felt good to be doing something and get away from the tension that was boiling over at the house. It was about a 20-minute ride. There wasn't much traffic or tourists in the area, and she arrived quickly. Most traffic was local, with it being off season. Lizzie arrived at the park, spotting Marcus waiting for her in the tree line. She pulled up and parked alongside him. He tenderly took her hand in his, a comforting sign of the friendship they had shared since childhood.

The beach area near the lifeguard stand had been closed off with police tape, blocking the pair from getting further access. A wave of panic washed over Lizzie, her pulse pounding in her ears, her mouth suddenly dry.

No one noticed the two kids on their bikes observing the police activity. A pair of deputies looked to be studying the area around the lifeguard stand, and another was sweeping the arms of the chair for fingerprints. "Geez," Marcus whispered. "Did your parents make the cops do a search? Don't they usually wait like 24 hours or something before people get to be missing?"

She knew what he meant, but just shrugged her shoulders, not wanting to share the full depth of the adult conversation in her kitchen. Doing so would make it more real. They both watched enough of the TV crime shows that they thought themselves to be pretty good at police procedure, TV police procedure, that is. "I don't know if they did or not."

"Likely," Marcus replied, nodding, self-assured and entitled.

He was right. After all the years of special treatment with Cami's infractions, the same was likely happening now. Because of her family's community stature, the police were taking this seriously.

"Look," Marcus whispered loudly. "They've got divers out there. That can't be good!"

Lizzie followed his line of sight to the water's edge, revealing divers in the shallow water, searching side by side. Some walked in water, others were swimming with dive gear on, all an arm's length from the other.

They were looking for her sister in the water. *In the water since this morning?*

Her gut sank and chills ran up her spine as she slowly realized what this meant. This was not just Cami running off somewhere. There was something more sinister at play. Did the police have a reason to believe she was in the water? *Her body?* Had someone had taken her or harmed her? *What had they found to make them think that?*

Lizzie's blood chilled in the 90-degree humidity. *Where was she?*

Marcus wrapped his arms around her as tears coursed down her cheeks. They watched in fascinated horror, hoping they found something, but dreading if they did.

It was too much. The reality of the situation crashed around her. Lizzie sank to her knees in the sand, unable to catch her breath. The world felt as though it was closing in. Her airway tightened in her chest as her vision narrowed. Marcus panicked and shouted to the group of searchers for help.

Minutes later, a cold, wet hand grasped her shoulder. "You shouldn't be here," a male voice said gruffly, thrusting a paper bag over her lips. It smelled of peanut butter. Probably had recently been used for someone's lunch. "Breathe, breathe. It's okay, I've got you."

Lizzie's eyesight turned to black and white, and she knew she would pass out in short order. Her rescuer blocked her view of the beach with his body, dressed in a wet suit,

"I can't believe you came here!" he admonished Marcus, standing anxiously nearby, pale and worried.

Marcus opened his mouth to retort, but apparently thought better of it. A rare move for her cousin. Slowly, as she calmed, Lizzie realized who had come to her rescue. He was familiar, but she'd never interacted this closely with Damen Wisler. The older brother of the Wisler treasure hunting family, her mother, advised her to avoid.

And now the sullen, dark, and older half-brother of Daniel Wisler, Marcus's golden-haired friend, had her in his grasp. Marcus and Daniel had referred to him as 'the beast' for his outbursts of anger at their antics. Lizzie was at his mercy as he urged her to 'breathe'. She was both awed and frightened of him and did as he instructed. In minutes, her breath came easier, the panic attack subsiding.

Damen's dark eyes assessed her for signs of passing out, and he released his grip from her shoulder but stayed close by. His focus on Marcus, "She needs to go home. Can you take her?"

Marcus's eyes widened. "We came on bikes."

Damen huffed, causing Marcus to step back. It was rare to see Marcus intimidated. Even in her anxious state, Lizzie couldn't help but feel intrigued. Marcus knew Damen and, for some reason, was cowed by him.

Lizzie knew they shouldn't be here and really wanted to leave, but riding her bike home now wasn't a great idea. She felt too weak to even contemplate peddling home in her current state.

"I'll take her. Her bike over there?" Damen said, looking toward the trees, his jaw working in his stern face. "I can fit one bike in my truck. You'll have to ride home."

Marcus nodded and helped her to her feet. "You okay, Lizzie? He's right, you shouldn't be here. We need to leave. He can bring you home. It'll be all right."

Wait. Marcus was leaving her with Damen? Lizzie felt her panic rise again.

As if he sensed her rising reluctance, Damen grabbed her arm, both supporting her and propelling her forward, away from the beach, away from the search for her missing sister.

He grabbed her bike as they passed it, one hand guiding the bike, the other guiding her forward. The move was effortless for his tall, muscular build. Soon they passed into the parking lot; Damen leaned her bike against a small ancient pickup truck and guided her gently but firmly into the passenger seat.

She heard him stow her bike in the back before getting into the driver's seat. The muffler less engine made a loud, rumbling noise as he drove from the parking lot. He didn't say a word on the drive to her house; the silence stretching between them. His dark hair dripping water on the worn seat cushions. Knowing he knew where she lived, she too was silent. They saw Marcus as he pedaled away, the late afternoon sun reflecting off his bike as he left the beach parking lot.

The sheriff's vehicle was still parked in their driveway. The reality of the situation engulfed her senses. A wave of overwhelming emotion, an invisible weight in the pit of her stomach, crashed into her. As a fourteen-year-old, it filled her with an intense fear and anxiety that she could not control. She felt like the walls were closing in around her, with the search on the beach, her parents' panic, and the sight of police cars outside her house. Tears ran down her cheeks uncontrollably as she sobbed.

Now mortified, Lizzie felt her heart sink as tears streamed down her face and her nose ran like a fountain in the older boy's car. If this news spread, it would ruin the chance of her going on a date before she was 40. Damen grasped her shoulders and pressed her against him. She could feel the dampness of his skin from the ocean, combined with the smell of salt and air. He patted her back soothingly. She'd never been in the arms of a boy, so she was at a loss to compare it to anything else. His embrace calmed her, wrapping her in safety and security.

Her tears kept coming until her throat was raw from the cries. By the time the emotional storm had passed, she was filled with a dull, aching pain in her gut. Lizzie had cried, unaware that it would be only the start of her grief for her sister. Damen held her until she calmed down, her face wet with tears and snot. He handed Lizzie his t-shirt to wipe her eyes, discarded earlier from when he changed into his wetsuit. "I don't have any tissue. I'm sorry."

Lizzie wiped her eyes and blew her nose into the shirt, and Damen winced. "Why don't you take that with you?" he said when she tried to hand it back to him.

It smelled of fresh air, grease, and something else she couldn't place. It was oddly comforting. Damen waited with her until she was ready to get out of the truck and go into the house, where her parents waited on news of her sister. It was a kindness from a virtual stranger who had taken the time to care for her while helping in the search for her missing sister.

She knew they all stuck together in the Keys to help one another, but this was a step further than neighborly kindness. It touched her, and she waved awkwardly as he pulled from the driveway, his discarded t-shirt clenched in her hands.

CHAPTER I

Her back muscles strained as she pushed the small tender from the back dive deck of her uncle's power catamaran yacht. Marcus guided the boat away before starting its small outboard engine, avoiding both the yacht and the salvage dive boat nearby. Daniel sat facing Marcus, organizing their fishing rods and gear, a floppy hat covering his sunny grin. Lizzie couldn't help but smile at the pair, waving as they pulled away. "Catch some fish for dinner!" she shouted, laughing after them.

They were a lot of fun to be around, and her closest friends, besides Ashley, her only close girlfriend. Marcus and Daniel were taking a few hours to fish the flats of the nearby atoll. It was a great idea for some activity during the lull in diving, and Lizzie was selfishly glad for some time for herself. The Marquesas Keys were uninhabited. Their shifting sands and shallow passages made it dangerous for boating, but great for fishing. It was a popular spot for sport fishermen and recreational boaters off the Florida Keys.

The treasure salvage project Daniel and his brother were working, along with the crew of the *Merchant,* had a lot of guesswork. Daniel referred to it as finding a needle in a haystack. The wrecks they were searching for had been lost in a hurricane in the 1600s. Having the maps from over 400 years ago and notes from other dives and research made the process a little easier, but it was still an arduous task. Their father's company had been searching for the *Atocha* for years, with very little to show. A gold coin here and there, enough to keep the interest going, but not enough to pay the bills.

So far, they had changed their location by a few hundred yards three times in the past few days. Divers would search around if the sonar equipment located an item of interest on the ocean floor. If nothing materialized, they shifted the search location. Today, they apparently felt close to something and were using the salvage ship's engines to 'blow a hole' in the sand. Essentially, using the motion of the engines to stir up the sand that would cover the wrecks or their cannons.

This procedure had been used by their father's salvage company for years and had gotten the attention and the ultimate approval of environmental groups. They had strict limitations and guidelines to follow when using the technique to minimize the impact on the environment.

Marcus and Lizzie weren't involved in the treasure hunt and had kept to the yacht to stay out of the way of everyone and away from Daniel's older brother, Damen, who disapproved of their presence. She hadn't interacted directly with the crew or Damen since they dropped anchor, leaving any communication to go through with Daniel.

Damen had complained voraciously to Daniel about his friends showing up on the dive site. He thought they were bored rich kids looking for something to do before heading back to their Ivy leagues. Her uncle's power catamaran yacht, although small and dated, displayed luxury and comfort next to the battle-worn, aging, and often malfunctioning *Merchant*. The salvage boat had bunks for 6 crew, with many more usually on board. Equipment and people covered the deck. Most of the crew slept outside at night, as Lizzie did, likely their cause was lack of air conditioning versus her nightly insomnia.

Lizzie sighed; she honestly couldn't disagree with Damen's assessment of them. Their families were well off, Marcus's more so than Lizzie's. So far, though, they had been of help when the food storage on the dive boat failed, and they needed to feed the crew. They shared their abundant food stores and extra storage space.

She wasn't just a typical rich kid with nothing to do; she was privately anxious and uneasy. It was so good to be out of the house and away from the silence of her parents' home. Their relationship had been strained since Cami disappeared. By the tension in the household, she assumed they were more vocal with each other when she was away at college withholding their fighting for her sake. The friction had become too much for her to deal with. Her father usually spent most of his time in Boston working as a college professor, taking in the summer break with Lizzie in Florida. The weather was crazy with the heat and humidity, but her mother refused to leave. They all needed to go to Florida for the summer, in order for them to be together as a family. The breezes from the Gulf and the Atlantic made it so not that bad.

Further separation and divorce were likely in her parent's future. It should bother her more than it did, but for her whole life, they'd always seemed like such an unlikely couple. She always thought they would be happier apart, especially her father, who was an outsider among the locals and her mother's family. Soledad was a challenging woman to have any kind of relationship with, disapproving and stern.

The silence and lack of emotion from her mother had creat-ed an impregnable barrier between the two of them. Lizzie knew she suffered, staying in the past, waiting for some news of her missing daughter. She simply wanted to be alone with her grief and exclude the rest of her family. The mystery of what had happened to her eldest child had eaten away at her, leaving her a shell of her former self.

Even though it had been years since Cami disappeared, it still hung around Lizzie like a heavy burden. A weight that everyone who knew her in Key West saw whenever they looked at her, the girl whose sister had gone missing. The same weight lifted somewhat whenever she left. Going away to college was a relief. She could leave the yoke behind and be herself, at least on the surface. Anxiety and dread nipped at her subconscious, rising to the surface in the night's quiet, disturbing most nights' sleep.

Lizzie continued to pursue answers and had hope of find-ing some information or evidence about Cami. Her parents had curbed her pursuit after it became an obsession in high school and continued to discourage her from it now. Engag-ing in finding answers had been a salve to her pain of losing her older sibling. It gave her a purpose and helped to con-trol her anxieties. She continued to research cases around the area, meeting with police and reviewing evidence when they permitted. Lizzie had wanted to do more and tried to change her major from pre-med to pre-law, but her father disapproved. His dream was for her to follow in his footsteps in medicine, and he would see that she did just that.

The police were not as helpful as one would assume they would be in this case. They didn't have answers she wanted and displayed frustration with her continued investigation. Recently, Paul Nichols, a high school classmate who worked part-time as a deputy and was studying criminal justice part time, was interested in helping to solve Cami's case. Lizzie wasn't completely naïve to the fact that he was most interested in her and unfortunately for him; she wasn't above meeting him for drinks or dinner in order to gain information.

The deputy's company was enjoyable enough, and they had a good time when together, so it wasn't a chore. She really appreciated the help he offered, but Lizzie wasn't interested in a relationship. The burdens of her parents' disintegrating relationship, Cami's disappearance, school, and that she was supposed to be in a relationship with Daniel hindered the growth of anything between her and the young deputy. This was one time Lizzie appreciated the façade of being Daniel's girlfriend. It made life less complicated. Only three people on the planet knew that their love affair was not what they played it out to be. Two of them had just gone fishing together.

It was great that Marcus and Daniel could be who they really were together, at least for a few hours. They, too, left a burden behind when not in Key West with their families. Neither Marcus nor Daniel had felt free to come out to their families. But they had a relationship away from them, and had been together for their college years, as most thought Daniel and Lizzie had. They were all due to graduate in the spring. Lizzie loved them both dearly, and Marcus was her best friend. It was natural for them to all be frequently together. Their fondness for each other was real, so there wasn't much more for anyone to observe unless they realized Lizzie slept alone. Something they were unlikely to observe on this trip. With just the three of them staying on the small yacht, their secrets were well kept.

The late morning sun grew hot, a trickle of sweat beaded on her brow as she burrowed her head into the deck chair, her back naked to the sun's rays. It felt glorious.

The 'blowers' from the dive boat the *Merchant* stopped. Silence echoed in the relative stillness of the Gulf waters. Lizzie drifted as sleep toyed with her mind. She never slept well on the water; the cramped cabin made her feel claustrophobic. It was a little ironic, feeling closed in on the open water. Instead, she spent most nights on the deck chair where she was now. It was comfortable enough and better than being in her parents' house.

Her breathing slowed as sleep overtook her thoughts, lulled by the lap of water on the hull.

Drops of cold water on her back startled her awake. *Was it raining? How long had she been asleep?* She sat bolt upright, forgetting momentarily the clasp of her bikini top was undone. She pulled her clothing clumsily covering her exposed breasts, and came face to face with Damen, sopping wet and leaning over her. Lizzie felt her stomach sink as she was overcome with embarrassment. *Had he seen me?* Her heart pounded, feeling like it was going to burst from her chest.

He was bigger than she remembered up close, lean and imposing. Tattoos scattered across his chest and arms added to his menacing air. She swallowed the hard lump that had risen in her throat, her face burning as he scowled.

"Where is he?" Damen asked, his voice a growl. He stood dripping sea water all over the deck with his scuba tanks strapped to his back.

She swallowed deeply before answering, trying to calm herself and get her bearings back from her nap. "They took the tender out to fish...."

"The hole's blown. We need all hands," he interrupted. "How long ago did they leave? When were they coming back? Dammit, he knew we'd need him."

He paced a few steps away from her, frustration seeping from his movements.

"I.... I don't know I was...." *God, he intimidates me! Why do I react so to him? The 'Beast' is such a suiting nickname for him,* she thought.

"Yeah, I know. You were taking a nap," he snapped.

He didn't need to tell Lizzie they dove in pairs after blowing the hole; she knew this from the years spent with his brother. The water would be murky with sand and sediment blown up from the bottom. It was a safety measure their father insisted upon after a diving accident years ago, where a crew member died.

An idea occurred to her, a wild and really unlikely idea. She knew Daniel and Marcus wouldn't be back for a while, and she loved to dive. Diving was a skill long learned for her, having taken it up in the years after Cami left to keep busy and out of the house. Ocean all around them and many willing dive instructors, Daniel included. Her gut reaction had her leaping at the chance to be one of the first down after they blew the sand away with the engines from the dive boat. Tales from the crew and Daniel of finding long buried treasure were intriguing. This time, hanging out with Daniel on site, albeit briefly, had caught her up in the fever that the treasure hunters lived on and kept them going for years, searching endlessly for lost treasure.

"I.... I can dive," she said, not quite believing her mouth was saying the words. She shifted from foot to foot, continuing to straighten her clothing. She'd was sure she flashed a full frontal, but he hadn't reacted. Not in the same way she was to him at the moment, bumbling all over herself, regressing right back to the chubby fourteen-year-old he'd been so kind to.

She tried to not appear too eager, for fear he'd change his mind and wait for Daniel to return, but only she knew they would take their time. They definitely wouldn't be back soon.

He seemed to hesitate, his eyes uncertain as he studied her as a potential dive partner. His eyes assessed her, feeling as though they bored into her skin. His appraisal sent a rush of excitement through her body, catching her off guard. Lizzie had a crush on Damen when she was younger, after he had rescued her from witnessing the search for her sister on the beach the day she disappeared. She thought it long dormant, but here she was.

It crossed her mind briefly, in a second of panic, to take back the offer. She'd be with *him*, and she hadn't been close to him or really spoken to him since the day Cami disappeared. When she and Daniel hung out, it was usually at Marcus's house, as they were largely unsupervised there. She hadn't been near Damen to speak of in years. Not that they'd be conversing under water, but he was making her edgy.

As he considered her, she allowed herself to gauge him. His eyes were shrouded in shadows, making it impossible for her to read what he was thinking. She was struck by how much he had changed - he was now a lot taller and thicker than she remembered. His broad chest was muscular and lean. His years in the Navy had added size, and in all the right parts. Her mind drifted as she took in his physique. Definitely a unique specimen than either Marcus or Daniel, who were athletic, but not in the way of Damen. He was a *man*, as her girlfriend Ashley would say.

"All right, get your gear on. We'll go off the starboard side. Stay together. It'll be murky down there. You can get disoriented if you're not used to it." A shadow passed over his face and he seemed to hesitate again.

This time, she knew what he was thinking; her parents didn't need to lose another kid.

She prepped quickly, eager to drop into the cooler water of the Gulf. Even though Damen intimidated her, she knew he'd watch out for her. From what she could see of him, which was plenty, he could fully fend off any predators. He continued to rattle off instructions while she readied her dive equipment, not bothering with a wet suit like most of the crew and Damen. He scrutinized her gear, checking valves and tanks.

"It's likely if we're in the right spot, we'll see the cannons first. Look for elongated structures, around six feet long. They may look dark still, but they're likely to be covered with barnacles and centuries of sand ... and not look like cannons at first."

She'd heard from Daniel about this search. There was an entire fleet sailing from Cuba loaded with treasure for the Spanish Government. There were tons of gold, silver and emeralds bound for Europe that were lost in the sandy bottom of the Gulf of Mexico not seen for centuries. It would be a virgin shipwreck, never disturbed by another human, unheard of in this day and age. The lost fortune had been enough to change history, impacting the Spanish government's ability to wage war or defend itself or its territories from other country's aggressions.

Damen and Daniel's father was a treasure hunter and salvager who had been hunting shipwrecks for years. Both men worked side by side with their father, college and armed services time aside, scouring the ocean floor for long-lost trinkets. Daniel joked it was their family time to be diving for gold. His father searched endlessly, pouring his own and investor money to give the searches all that they had. Rarely, it had come to fruition. When it did, there had been big finds as it had several years prior on the Eastern side of Florida. Apparently, those treasure finds were funding this search, along with investor money. Lizzie knew funds were tight now for the company. Daniel complained that the equipment was old and breaking down. They really needed to find this treasure soon, to pay the bills.

Once Damen was satisfied with her gear, they dropped into the water side by side. Lizzie keeping close to Damen's side as they slowly descended through the murky water. He hadn't been kidding that diving in these conditions would be dangerous. For the second time she second guessed her choice to dive with him.

Her eyes adjusted as the sunlight faded into the deeper waters of the surrounding shallow sea. The water cooled her skin, initially feeling wonderful compared to the surface heat. After a few minutes, she questioned the wisdom of not wearing her wetsuit.

As they moved through the water, Lizzie's mind shifted to the shipwrecks and the lives that were lost so long ago, having no chance against a hurricane. While it was unlikely to find any human remains, she still felt as though they were trespassing on a grave.

CHAPTER 2

Everything had been going wrong with this trip ever since they'd left port. It was enough for him to question any consideration of ever leaving the service to work for his father. This extended leave, long overdue vacation, was intended for relaxation. His team had been operating nearly non-stop for months, and he was close to burning out. The entire team was on edge, especially after the death of a colleague on their last unsuccessful mission. It had gutted Damen, causing him to step back and re-think his career choice in the SEALs. It had been his lifelong dream, but it left little time for anything outside of work.

His father, Isaac, expected him to spend his time at home in pursuit of treasure. He was more driven than usual, certain they were close to finding the treasure of the *Atocha*. The manifest of the ship was supposedly full of silver, gold and emeralds. Its passengers were aristocrats, and church royalty who carried personal treasures and gold. The potential value had his father practically manic.

This trip out on the salvage boat with his little brother, Daniel, and the crew searching, endlessly searching for the *Atocha*, had really gotten him to think clearly about his future. It didn't involve this. This work had been his father's dream. Damen had been born into it, and compelled to work at it alongside his father, but it wasn't his dream. It never had been.

His father, who has searched for years and years for millions and millions of lost gold and treasure in the shipwrecks off the coast of Florida, had come to the end of his funding. The equipment they were using showed it. The *Merchant* was a failing rust bucket. They had trouble with the deck winch engine and food storage, to name a few of the things that were breaking down. They had rigged the bilge pumps countless times. Getting them to function was nothing short of a miracle.

It was incredibly annoying that the equipment was unreliable, and it was the most irritated he'd had ever been on a trip. Understandably, he realized he was likely more agitated because his life's work was elsewhere. Adding to his frustration, his little brother Daniel and his girlfriend had been floating nearby in a yacht living in the lap of luxury while he crammed into crew quarters without air conditioning and to search for gold that they'd probably never find.

Damen knew he was envious of his brother's college-boy ways and normal life, with friends and a steady girl. Daniel's golden-haired, fun-loving persona was so unlike Damen's seriousness that it caused the men challenges over the years. Damen loved his little half-brother, but he'd always felt himself the outsider with his family. Daniel was easier going, and easier to love.

Their father had been married several times. His first wife was Damen's mother, who died when he was born. Damen had always felt his father resented him because his life caused hers to end, although he'd never spoken of it. The *Golden Boy* Daniel had brought him joy and pride, whereas Damen had not.

However, Damen was the one that his father trusted to be in charge of his operations. Isaac had not been silent about wanting him to take over the business someday. That's why he was out there, again, searching for lost gold on his first leave in 2 years, because his father needed him.

The morning was heating up, and with the hole blown in the sand, it was time for them to dive. Daniel was nowhere to be found. Already angry, Damen took seconds to swim over to the yacht Daniel had been partying on with his friends while he sweated his ass off.

He didn't expect to find what he found on the deck of the power catamaran.

A visceral animal ache punched him in the gut, stunned to realize who he was looking at. Damen stood dumbfounded, dripping water everywhere and on *her*. This was not the chubby, acne tortured girl he remembered.

There, lying in the deck chair, sound asleep, was a gorgeous specimen of a woman. Long athletic and tanned legs topped a firm derriere. Followed by a long stretch of silky skin to a rumpled pile of wild, windblown hair. His brother's long-time girlfriend, Elisabeth, better known as Lizzie, was half naked and sound asleep.

Apparently, he'd been away a while, and not taken an interest in Daniel's life. Damen had not paid attention in his anger when these brats showed up on the dive site. He would have remembered if Daniel had mentioned *her. Had he?*

His silent dripping presence startled her, and she jumped up, momentarily forgetting her unfastened bikini top. *There is a God!* Her revelation rendered him speechless. The most beautiful half- naked woman he'd seen stood before him. He wanted to react the way his body was calling him to, but he couldn't or wouldn't.

Instead, he did what he always had, frown and make no move. It always worked well for him to intimidate instead of react. Damen knew that others often referred to him as "the beast" from this intimidation tactic and his unrestrained outbursts whenever he was displeased. He didn't mind, it actually suited him.

Damen and Lizzie have a brief exchange and somehow, he found himself agreeing to have her dive with him, because Daniel was nowhere to be found. He knows she has dive skills because she has been diving periodically with Daniel and he has spoken about *that*. However, in his gut, he felt like this was probably not a wonderful idea. It's likely an idiotic idea on his part. He would end up watching out for her and worrying about whether she was safe rather than searching for the gold they'd come here to find. He didn't have time for this, nor the patience to deal with this kind of inexperience.

But he said nothing.

She was eager, and pretty. He let it slide at least this one time. They were burning daylight and needed to get going. Damen felt a weird sensation in his gut, a feeling that today might be the day they found something to pay the bills. Money was the constant worry for this operation. Enough for supplies, the payroll, and all the things that Damen really didn't want to be worrying about.

He gave her brief instructions about looking for cannons and maintaining safety. She paid attention; he'd give her that. As they descended into the murky water, she was the only thing that he could focus on. Damen took a moment to appreciate her God given female gifts as they descended to the bottom of the sea. *Seriously dude, get hold of yourself.*

They could see through the cloudy water where the *Merchant's* engines blew the sand in the target area. All the silt and ocean debris that had sat at the bottom for decades, if not centuries, floated around them. Thankfully, his new dive partner stayed close and watched him carefully as they examined the ocean floor beneath their fins.

As his eyes adjusted to the murky water, Damen noted a large, elongated dark form on the ocean floor, visible through the murkiness of the disturbed sand. His heart pounded in his chest as he realized that this could be one of the elusive cannons they'd been searching for. Damen motioned to Lizzie to stay with him as he moved closer. Together, they carefully fanned their hands over the dark form, revealing what appeared to be a cannon.

Excitement ran through his veins as he immersed himself in inspecting their find, not paying attention to Lizzie as she moved in his peripheral vision. The cannon was very dark, appearing to be a bronze cannon that would have come from a ship in the era the *Atocha* went down. *Bronze!* If he was right, and this was a cannon from that time, it would be a rare and valuable find. His father would be very pleased. Damen was glad to have something finally go right on this dive.

In the back of his mind, he considered the damaged winch above and wondered how soon it would take to get it repaired so they could hoist the cannon up onto the deck of the *Merchant*.

While his mind raced, his eyes caught Lizzie swimming a few yards away. He could barely make her out through the murky water. She was fanning hands quickly over the sand, her motions growing in urgency.

Damen saw it at the same time Lizzie did. The glitter of an object bouncing in the murky light. She startled, quickly grabbing the item and brought it to her face for inspection.

Frantically, she waved to him, holding the object in her hand. Damen swam immediately to her side.

Gold! A small gold coin glittered in her hand. They'd found gold! There had to be more! Damen took it from her to examine, excitedly embracing her under the water. His eyes scanned the seabed where she'd found the object, and he found himself dumfounded for the second time today, his heart pounding against his ribs. Several gold coins lay scattered across the ocean floor, trickling a path to where the ship's engines had blown the hole in the sand. Timbers of decaying wood lay opened like the carcass of a whale before them. Lumps of likely additional buried objects lay strewn across the sand, covered in barnacles and growth. Damen struggled to regulate his breathing.

Could this be the mother lode that his father had been searching for decades? Could this be the millions and millions of dollars of gold, emeralds and silver supposed to be in the Atocha's hold? Is this the treasure?

Excitedly, Lizzie and Damen picked up the scattered coins, putting them in his dive bag. Taking care to rise slowly to the surface, they ascended crazily, excited. As soon as their heads broke the surface, they screamed and yelled to the rest of the crew. They sounded like sharks were killing them, causing everyone on the surface to rush to their aid. Instead, they heard what every treasure hunter across the world wanted to hear on every day and every dive.

We've found gold!

CHAPTER 3

Lizzie was so excited about finding the gold at the bottom of the ocean that she couldn't contain herself. The thrill and excitement were something she hadn't felt in a very long time. The response of the crew on the *Merchant* was crazy as they realized what Damen and Lizzie were saying. They'd found gold!

The entire crew was in the water in an instant. They were all diving, free diving, or diving with scuba gear to see what they had found at the bottom of the ocean. It was mayhem!

Damen and Lizzie dove back down, with Damen gripping her hand, shaking it as he excitedly pointed to the objects below. To Lizzie, there were lumps in the sand, but they were *something* to him and the crew. *Something huge!*

It was very curious that no one was moving objects and taking anything more than the few coins they'd collected to the surface. Nobody was picking anything more up from the bottom. Even though there were items scattered around the seabed floor, readily and easily available. From where they'd picked up the gold coins, there were stacks of what appeared to be long, heavily encrusted logs piled up on the ocean floor. Sea life covered the bricks. Lobsters had made themselves a home in the scattered debris of the sunken Spanish galleon. These objects really caught the attention of Damen and the crew, and they all floated above them, looking in awe at the area.

The longer they studied the objects scattered below, the more she realized what the excitement was about. As her brain put together the forms beneath, the skeleton hull of the ship formed before her eyes. The embedded the timbers of a floating ship protruded in the deep sand. Its cannons scattered about where they had landed centuries ago. They'd located the wreck that had been lost and buried underneath the sand for four centuries. It was a wonder to behold.

After a while of looking at their find, their air supply ran low, and they needed to surface. Once back at the surface, Lizzie followed Damen aboard the rusty, dilapidated *Merchant*. The deck buzzed with excitement and activity.

"Come on," Damen said, pulling her by the hand. He was excited and happy, unlike his previous sullen persona. "I need to call my father."

She struggled to keep up with him over the maze of equipment and excited crew on the deck, puzzled why he pulled her along with him, his high spirits making him seem crazed. Once they arrived at the bridge, Damen made a call on the radio.

"Dad, Dad.... Are you sitting down?" he shouted into the ship's radio.

There's a heavy silence. "Is this good news or bad?" Isaac Wisler answered, his gravel voice distinctive, made so by years of cigars and alcohol.

"We've found it, I'm certain. It's a big school of fish!"

The radio crackled as they waited for the older man to respond. "No."

Laughter and excitement exploded through the radio and suddenly cut off. Damen squeezed her hand tightly, shaking it excitedly and smiling widely. "They're crazed!" he said. "The entire office has got to be out of their minds!"

Isaac Wisler kept a working office near the docks and another in the family's maritime treasure museum, where Isaac displayed objects found in previous wrecks. Daniel spoke often of the geographic ease his father had to walk downtown to any of the local bars and was often to be found there. An activity the older man had taken advantage of after the death of Daniel's mother several years ago.

After a moment, Isaac's voice came back on the radio. "So, what you're saying, son, is that the fishing is *real* good today?"

Damen shrugged at Lizzie's puzzled expression. "Yes sir! I think you should ask Pierre Hardin if he'd like to come join us. I know he was looking for a chance to catch some good ones."

"That sounds just fine, son. We can be out there by the morning. Why don't you all rest up tonight?"

"Sounds good, 10-4," Damen replied practically giddy. He hung up the microphone and then grabbed Lizzie, his arms wrapping around her in a tight hug, his hands gently resting on her shoulders. Instantly, her heart rate quickened as she felt the warmth of his firm, masculine body against her. The energy between them was palpable, like a jolt of electricity ran through their veins. His eyes suddenly stony, he quickly pushed her away, his large hands gripping her upper arms. Her heart thumped loudly in her chest, echoing in her ears. She was sure he could hear it. *What was that?*

Lizzie stepped back, causing Damen's arms to fall to his side, his expression changing back to his familiar scowl. "Sorry Lizzie, I got carried away...."

She changed the subject. "I'm confused. Why would your dad come out to go fishing? Didn't we just find the wreck?"

Damen's expression changed back his earlier mirth. "Oh no, no," he laughed, moving further away from her in the cramped space. "He knows it's a big deal. He'll be out here by morning with the archeologist who needs to supervise the recovery. Anyone can overhear what we are saying on that radio. We'll want to not publicize that we may have found the motherlode. Every Tom, Dick and Harry will be out here before nightfall, looking to claim a piece. Security's a big issue."

Awareness dawned on her. Of course, they wouldn't want the world to know what they may have just found feet beneath the ship. The thought of drug smugglers with machine guns sent a chill down her spine. They sailed in these waters, smuggling goods from South and Central America and Cuba. *Who knows how much treasure they just came across and who else would be interested in it?*

"Is that how come no one was bringing anything else up?"

Damen laughed out loud, the sound joyous. This discovery had the entire crew giddy, but something had stymied them from gathering anything more than the few coins they brought up. She would have thought they'd all be down there; pulling up whatever they could find.

His expression changed as he appeared to think about how to answer her question. Brows furrowed as he looked out the window overlooking the deck and the crew below. Someone had turned on a portable stereo. Music blared through mini speakers scattered over the deck. Beers had appeared, officially banned during normal operations, but entirely appropriate now, considering the circumstances.

"We have to have an archaeologist supervise the excavation for this type of wreck because it helps to preserve its history. It's really like a time capsule of sorts, sitting down there, untouched for centuries. If we went digging through the wreckage to pull up all the coins and everything that we see down there, we risk damaging any history that may be part of what we're trying to recover. And it can provide a look into life then.

"My father started a policy of having an archaeologist on staff to keep the integrity of the treasure. It's an added expense, but it's kept the regulators off his back." Damen turned and looked at her, his expression serious. "Before he did that people used to refer to his crews as 'pillagers' of the ocean. Taking valuable treasure items from wrecks, destroying the history of the objects underneath the ocean. Having credential on staff really helped discourage that view."

They stood silent for a few moments. His broad back to her as he looked out on the deck, his mind elsewhere. The earlier happiness dispersed, and his shoulders seemed to slump as she watched. It didn't last long, making Lizzie wonder if she imagined it.

She felt a chill run down her spine as he approached her, his enormous frame a looming presence. He bent down in front of her, his arm brushing against her calf, and reached past her legs. Immediately Lizzie felt exposed her half naked bikini-clad body, and a shiver prickled her skin.. He hesitated, as if he realized the same.

"Ahh.... I'm sorry," he apologized, glancing up to look into her face, her stomach dropping as their eyes met. She stood there for a brief moment, her nerves turning to jelly. Then she realized he was pointing under her foot.

"There's a cooler, just under... ah... there..."

Her face burned; likely coloring her face crimson. Their eyes meet again. This time Lizzie was certain she could feel his breath on her thigh. She froze.

Slowly, as though contemplating his actions, his large hand grasped her knee. Immediately, she felt the heat of his hand on her skin, like a roaring inferno. He slowly let go of her as one finger delicately ran along the inside of her calf, from her knee to the delicate arch of her heel.

Her heart skipped a beat. She held her breath, unsure of what to do.

He grasped her ankle in his large palm, holding it momentarily, while the heat from his skin burned hers. He lifted her foot, moving it back from its position. She exhaled slowly.

He flipped a latch on the floor where she'd been standing, and the floor opened, revealing a lid to a hidden compartment. "This is where we keep the champagne and booze. You know, just in case."

Instantly, Lizzie was mortified. *Had she read into his touch?* She scolded herself for reacting like a hormonal teenager.

Damen gathered several bottles of champagne that were kept hidden away in the concealed cooler. Standing, he shoved them into her still trembling hands. "Can you manage these?" he asked. "I'll grab some mugs from the galley."

Her arms full of bottles; he placed the last flask of champagne on top of the others in her arms, brushing both his hands down her upper arms, leaving a trail of goose pimples behind.

Lizzie realized this was *not* her imagination. He was purposefully touching her, and she was very attracted to him. Being a fake girlfriend to a closeted gay man had its perks. Exposure to virile hetero-sexual men wasn't one of them. She didn't know him well and wasn't so sure that this wasn't his *way* with women. She rationalized she was his little brother's girl, so he may take that familiarity a little further because of the celebratory mood. But she wasn't the chubby

14-year-old that she was the last time they'd interacted this closely.

Not sure how to react, Lizzie quickly exited the com, with six bottles of champagne rattling in her arms as she strode back on deck. The crew cheered when they saw what she was carrying. Corks started popping as the bottles disappeared from her grip. The last one going into Damen's hands.

"A toast!" one of the crew shouted. "To our lucky charm!"

The crew and Damen all toasted her. She felt her face blush like mad. "No, no!" she cried out. "I've never been on a treasure dive before. I've done nothing. Here's to you all for the work you've done on this project!"

A roar went up among the small dive team as they voraciously consumed champagne and beer. Happiness was all around as the celebration continued through the afternoon, under the later afternoon sky. They passed the coins that Lizzie and Damen had found around the small crowd, each marveling at the pieces, likely eager to dive for more.

Lizzie marveled at the group that had spent day after day out on water searching for gold. They appeared to be a rough crowd, mostly men, with tattoos, scars, and unkempt hair and beards. There were some familiar faces, and some that she didn't know. Through Daniel, she was familiar with some of their back stories. If she hadn't known of them under different circumstances, she would have avoided them for fear of her safety. They were rough on the outside, but decent, hard-working people. Looking for their own big break of finding treasure.

It was ironic that the first time she dove with them was when they found the mother lode. It would have been Daniel had he been there. She had nothing to do with it, of course, just in the right place at the right time.

Damen grabbed the rowdy group's attention, reporting that the archaeologist would be on site, along with his father, as soon as the morning. "It'll give you all the time to sober up," he joked. "Remember to keep radio silent about our find. No calls, no texts, no social media–of course we don't have signals and internet... Just saying we don't want to attract any trouble out here," Damen said, his tone serious. "We'll get security figured out once we know for certain what we are dealing with.".

The crew gathered around at Damen's words. His announcement wasn't a surprise to the group. It was apparent they already knew the need to hold off reporting the discovery. Most nodded seriously. They were all more aware of security concerns than Lizzie was. Their significant expressions revealed their own worries. She overheard a few comments about problems lately with immigrants coming in boats, and the pirates that guided them.

Breaking through the music of the celebration, they could hear a man shouting from a distance. Everyone shifted their attention to the sound. Someone shut off the music as they strained to hear. "Someone's hurt!" a crew member called out, as he ran to the water's edge. It was Andy, a younger and wilder member of the crew. Daniel had shared that he was a surfer from California, turned treasure hunter. He could hold his breath the longest of the team, was the only other thing Lizzie knew of him.

It was apparent by how he ran the short distance that he had some to drink and was feeling it pretty well. He jumped over the dive deck and into the water, the back of his head cracking loudly against the dive ladder. Everyone winced. Her heart leaped in her throat at the sound of the man's skull hitting the metal. Even Lizzie knew that was a dangerous step. His jump had not given him enough air to make it cleanly over the rail.

Damen and another crew member jumped into the calm water after him. Moments passed, and no one surfaced. The remaining crew and Lizzie gathered near the di ve deck, ropes and life rings readied.

A skiff came into view from around the yacht, several feet away, with Marcus piloting. A prone figure lay in the boat at his feet. Her heart leaped in her throat. Daniel? *What had happened?*

Damen and the other man surfaced, holding an unconscious Andy's head above the water. Blood poured from the back of his head, swirling in the water surrounding the swimmers. They swam with their victim the short distance to the small yacht. Its low dive deck making it easier to get out of the water without having to maneuver the unconscious man up a ladder. Marcus steered the skiff behind them, docking next to the men as they pulled Andy from the water, his head dripping blood.

Without thinking through what she was doing, Lizzie scooted down the *Merchant's* dive ladder and swam the yards to the yacht to help. As she neared the dive deck, a large hand grabbed her arm and pulled her right out of the water as though she were a rag doll.

Damen growled at her as her feet found purchase. "What were you thinking?" he said, pointing at the water she'd just crossed. The sight of a shark's fin where she had been sent her stomach into freefall. The predator had wasted no time searching out the area with the blood in the water. Likely it had been in the area already investigating the activity and churn from the *Merchant's* blowers.

Seeing that the injured Andy was rousing and was being tended to by Damen and the other crewman. She helped Marcus with the tender, reaching in to touch Daniel's cheek. "What's happened?" she asked, relieved when Daniel responded to her touch.

"Just a little fall," he answered weakly.

"He fell and landed hard on his leg and some rusted metal. He's cut pretty badly. The bleeding's stopped. He might have broken his leg. I heard something snap, and he passed out cold." Marcus nervously wiped his brow, his hands shaking. "I thought he.... he..."

Lizzie touched Marcus's shoulder. "Do you have a first aid kit?" Damen asked authoritatively, stepping in to examine his little brother.

Nodding, she hustled and located the first aid box, hoisting it from its storage and bringing it to the swim deck. By the time she returned, Damen and Marcus had moved Daniel from the tender and transferred him to a deck chair. Damen examined his brother's leg, and Lizzie was relieved to see that Daniel was talking, but drowsy. With Daniel in one chair and Andy in the other, the area resembled a makeshift ER.

"Did he hit his head?" Damen asked, watching concerned as Daniel nodded off.

"No, he was in so much pain I gave him one of my Xanax," Marcus replied, shrugging apologetically. "I had to get him into the boat. It wasn't easy."

Damen opened the drawers of the first aid kit, digging through as if searching for something in particular. He exhaled. "Can you help me? I want to get a better look at his leg, see if we need to call air rescue."

"I called them from the reef. They're six hours out. There was a nasty accident at the 7-mile bridge and all units were engaged. We can get in pretty quickly with this boat, if we cook it. It's calm enough I can clock up the knots... Two-hour trip easily," Marcus replied.

Such were the rescue options out here two to three hours out from any civilization. They all knew the risks of living and working on the water, but now it was right in their faces. Lizzie was glad that things weren't more serious, or they'd be in big trouble.

Damen began taking down the makeshift bandage on Daniel's leg, causing him to cry out, rousted from his nap. "Let Lizzie do it, dammit, Damen. She's pre-med. I want to keep what's left of my skin!"

Lizzie repositioned herself beside Damen, shoulder to shoulder with the larger man. She gently pulled off the makeshift bandages Marcus had placed, being careful to not trigger more bleeding. Damen didn't move away as she peeled off the bloodstained t-shirt used to stem the blood flow. Lizzie was shocked at the state of Daniel's leg. There was a deep cut with blood continuing to ooze from it, with what looked like rusted specks of metal embedded in the wound. His leg was badly swollen. Damen and Lizzie exchanged a meaningful glance. It was obvious he needed medical attention soon. Infection could set in quickly. He was very lucky that the metal didn't damage a major vessel.

"Can you stand?" Damen asked.

Daniel shook his head. "I can't step on it."

"I can attest to that," Marcus muttered. "I still don't know how I got you into the boat. Adrenaline, maybe?"

"Daniel, when's the last time you had a tetanus shot?" Lizzie asked, concerned about what could already be festering in the wound.

"When I got stitches, you remember that, Damen?"

"You mean on the *Margarita?* When I stitched you up?" Damen answered. "That was a while ago... not since then?"

Lizzie dug through the first aid kit. There were tons of bandages and other items. She found what she was looking for, an emergency shot of penicillin. Further inspection of its contents revealed aspirin and sunburn cream. She made a mental note to talk to her father about the contents of the kit. Obviously, there was a need for more than what he'd authorized as the family doctor. "Damen, do you have any tetanus or novocaine on the *Merchant?*"

Damen sighed and pulled his hands through his short hair. "No, we're due to be re-supplied. I used the last tetanus a few days ago."

Lizzie subtlety motioned to Daniel's wound, watching Damen's eyes take in the specks of metal. "Can you get them out?" he asked.

"Not without novocaine. They're pretty deep. He needs the ER, and maybe a surgeon," she whispered.

Damen stood and motioned for Marcus to join him. They conversed softly, urgently discussing their next steps. Lizzie gently wrapped a clean bandage around Daniel's leg and administered the penicillin, knowing he wasn't allergic. He kissed her hand, obviously still buzzing from Marcus's sedative. Lizzie moved to tend to Andy, his head held by the other crew member, Eric, who had jumped into the water after Andy with Damen. Andy's eyes were glassy, and he appeared to be dazed. Lizzie thought he was likely to have a concussion and needed stitches.

After she was certain she'd done everything she could for the injured men, she joined the conversation between Marcus and Damen. "Let's leave now. I've gotten Andy's bleeding to stop, but I'm sure he's concussed."

The three men moved Daniel and Andy to the salon/kitchen area, where they could rest out of the elements while they were underway. If they were to make time, they would be more comfortable out of the wind and the noise of the engines.

After a brief discussion, Damen and Eric took the tender back to the *Merchant*. Shakily, Marcus prepped to get the boat underway, making Lizzie worry about his capability to maneuver the boat at the speeds he was referring to. She could help, but she didn't have the experience he had in piloting the yacht.

A noise on the dive deck surprised her as Damen returned with the tender and tossed a small bag onto the deck. He secured the small boat in its hold and joined the group in the cabin. He caught Lizzie's surprised expression as Marcus fired up the engines and they got underway. "I'm heading in. Two injured crew are my responsibility. And we're going to need more help if they can't work. I have some recruiting to do."

"What about the treasure?" she asked. Under the circumstances, she couldn't see leaving what may be a huge find, but she understood. He took his responsibilities seriously.

"Wait, what are you talking about?" Daniel asked, piping up at their conversation.

"We found it, little brother!" Damen exclaimed, patting Daniel's shoulder.

Realization to Damen's meaning moved across his face, and Daniel grinned. "You're kidding me! That's awesome!" His expression changed to a frown as he considered the situation. "Dammit! Now I've got a cut up leg!"

"Still will be plenty to see when you're back on your feet, little brother," Damen said.

"That much?" Daniel asked.

"That much," Damen replied.

"Whoa," Daniel exclaimed, settling back on the pillows.

The two men beamed at each other as the power catamaran built up to its cruising speed and skimmed over the water, both giddy with the prospect of treasure.

"Is Dad coming out?" Daniel asked. "He's going to be pissed if you're not there, man."

Damen walked out on the deck, the water streaming past as they sped across the ocean. Lizzie watched him as he looked out over the horizon, the muscles in his jaw working. She knew through Daniel that the relationship with his father was a rough one.

As Daniel drifted off, Lizzie's mind raced with thoughts of Damen and the harrowing events that had unfolded in the few hours since she'd agreed to dive with him. Two serious injuries and a heart-stopping encounter with a shark - it was certainly a run of ill-fate. A nagging question lingered in her mind; had they unwittingly unearthed a curse along with the long sought-after treasure?

Lizzie quickly dismissed the idea, feeling almost as though she were channeling her 'psychic' friend Ashley. *Don't be ridiculous!*

CHAPTER 4

Damen collapsed in the seat next to Marcus, where he piloted the power catamaran across the green-blue sea. They were really cooking along, just as Marcus had said they would. Damen admired how the power cat could really crank up the knots! He was in awe of the luxury of the small yacht. There was so much convenience and comfort jammed into the vessel that it was a little surprising, even for someone as experienced as Damen. He'd seen his share of yachts and all manner of boats but hadn't really spent any time on a catamaran yacht.

He admitted to himself that he was a little jealous of his brother, staying on this boat with his girlfriend and best friend. They were living in the lap of luxury and working air conditioning, while the rest of the crew suffered in the malfunctioning rust bucket.

Lizzie sat across from him; her lap full of his brother's head as she comforted Daniel. She whispered to him, attempting to make him feel better as they got closer to shore. Andy was still pretty dazed from hitting his head, making Damen more worried about him right now than about Daniel, even with his nasty cut. Andy likely had a serious concussion; a brain injury was definitely more worrisome. As soon as they were close enough to shore, Damen planned to radio in for a rescue squad to meet them at the dock.

He seriously doubted either of the men could dive over the next few weeks based on the extent of their injuries. This was terrible news, both for them and for the recovery of the treasure. He thought of the shark that had nearly grazed Lizzie after she recklessly jumped into the water with Andy's blood filling the area. Their activity earlier in the day already had attracted the sharks, and they really needed to be careful to begin with. The blood would have made them crazed. The near miss scared him.

Everything that could go wrong had gone wrong with this trip. The weight of the responsibility for all of them felt heavy in his chest. He was responsible for their safety on the ship and the dive site. This was one of the reasons that he didn't want to do this work for the rest of his life. Being a part of a special ops team whose purpose was to be in risky places for noble reasons was an entirely different matter than being on a dive sight hunting for elusive treasure. Putting life and limb at risk to *maybe* find something valuable wasn't worth it.

Damen was still processing what they'd found on the ocean floor. It was surreal after all the years of searching. Isaac had searched for this particular treasure well before Damen joined the Navy, now six-years in. The treasure that had sat there for centuries, evading his father and others as to its whereabouts.

The run of bad luck since they came near the wreck stirred superstitious thoughts. It was as though the ghosts of the *Atocha* cursed them for finding its treasure, wanting to stay hidden. It started with the boat losing power and then, once that was repaired, losing the food storage locker power, and the winch motor. Everything had gone wrong and now this!

Damen understood his father didn't have the finances to support the dive and invest in the equipment upkeep. This was most likely the cause of the equipment failures, rather than some curse. His father's company had been looking for the wrecks for years and patience has been wearing thin with the investors, leaving them to continue the search with the dilapidated boat and equipment. But now having injured divers would leave him with a skeleton crew, creating more challenges with the dive. Not being able to disclose what they'd found for security would make it harder to recruit any willing divers. Damen feared he wouldn't be able to find replacements, but he'd try once we get on shore.

He knew he was taking this all too seriously, leaving in a few weeks to get back to his life in Virginia Beach. This wasn't his rodeo. But he knew now that they had finally found the treasure, it would be his father's chance to have some success after working at it for so long. Damen felt responsibility and ownership in making sure the recovery of the wreck would go smoothly. Even though he was technically on vacation, he'd agreed to oversee the salvage operation and he took it seriously.

Once they were close to a half hour out, Damen made the radio call for the rescue squad to meet them at the dock. He used the name of Marcus's yacht, knowing that his father would be unlikely to get wind of this disaster just yet. Damen would prefer to let him know in person and while standing over the massive treasure they've just found. Isaac would be less likely to be as upset with him and his failings if he had a plan in place to address them at the same time, he broke the news of the decimated crew.

Damen marveled to himself about still wanting to please his father, even now as a grown man. The influence his father's approval had over him, even after all these years, was powerful. He wanted to please him and gain that elusive approval Isaac rarely dished out.

Once they got ashore, Damen planned for Marcus, Lizzie, and himself to follow the injured to the hospital in an Uber. He was sure Lizzie would want to be with Daniel, by the way she was babying him. A vision of laying his own head in her lap sent a pang of jealousy into his gut. *Where was this stuff coming from? She was his brother's girlfriend. He didn't need a relationship in his life or someone to care for him, or did he?* Daniel surely was appreciating the female caring attention he was receiving at the moment.

Once they arrived onshore and docked the boat, they found the ambulance waiting for them, drawing attention from other crew and sailors in the immediate area. They hustled to get Daniel transferred from the boat into the rescue squad. Not able to walk, they had to transfer him to a stretcher to get him off of the boat. Damen was once again grateful for the use of the yacht with its ease of docking and boarding.

Just as Andy got up to walk into the waiting ambulance, he slouched to the side, passing out cold steps from the rescue squad. Giving them all another bit of excitement on this disastrous trip. Damen was relieved they came ashore with him when they did. Instead of having Andy lose consciousness miles offshore, he was here in the care of medical professionals when it happened. The incident made Damen wonder if his condition was more serious. After all, he hit his head pretty hard when he jumped off the boat.

Maybe there is a curse on that wreck after all.

The fluorescent lighting of the hospital waiting room didn't detract from her beauty. Damen shook the thought away. He shouldn't be noticing his brother's girlfriend at all. Lizzie had taken a few minutes to throw on clothes, instead of wearing her bikini, into the hospital. The clothing did nothing to conceal the female shape Damen had been admiring for the past few hours.

Get a grip! It had been a long time since he'd had any female company. It was definitely not something on his priority list. He wasn't looking for a relationship, at least one that lasted more than one night. He'd need a break from being on the dive site for that to happen, and now locating the *Atocha*'s treasure would put a damper on much of that until his leave ended; and then there was deployment.

He exhaled deeply. His love life comprised a long series of dry spells. The longest in recent memory being the one he was in at the moment, and likely the reason he found himself attracted to his little brother's girl. Damen reflected Lizzie wasn't his type at all, preferring the bustier blonde. Lizzie was the exact opposite, with her dark hair and athletic build.

Damen had spent the time in the waiting room making calls to several other divers to see whether they'd be available immediately to come out and work on the wreck. But as he expected, many of them were still waiting for late paychecks or didn't really want to work on a boat with broken equipment. Word had gotten around that Isaac's crew was having challenges.

Obviously, he couldn't reveal they had found treasure, which would have definitely changed their minds. But he couldn't let word get out about it until they had the full breadth of the treasure and security worked out. That would take days to weeks to coordinate. Any diver would be more than willing to work with them once word got around of their find. For now, they would have to figure it out and work the small crew they had left really hard. Doubts crept into his thoughts about how they were going to get the work done, with breaking equipment and a partial crew. There would be a lot of tedious archaeological work to complete before they could bring up the treasure. The entire project would take patience, something not in his nature. He was used to taking on the mission, getting it done, and going home.

Antsy, he paced around the waiting room. It was remarkably empty, reflecting the slower off-season population. Lizzie and Damen were the only two people in the room after a small family cleared out a short time ago.

It surprised him that Lizzie had stayed out there with him, instead of in the examination room with Daniel, holding his hand and making him feel better. Instead, Marcus was back with Daniel; they were only allowing one visitor with the patient. They'd been like the three musketeers for a long time, but it puzzled him why she was preferring to sit in the waiting room instead of in the examination room with her boyfriend. "Not a fan of hospitals?" he asked. "You seemed to have things in hand earlier..."

She smiled up at him from scrolling through her phone. "Oh, well." She appeared as if she were trying to find what to say, and Damen felt his radar go up. *Was she lying?* "I don't mind hospitals, really. I've spent enough time in them with my father."

Damen sat heavily in the chair across from her. Of course, her father was a surgeon. "Oh, right... Daniel said you were pre-med?"

A blush crept into her cheeks. "Yes. I guess I have to work on my bedside skills. I'm not very patient about waiting. Marcus is much better at it than I am."

"You seemed pretty good comforting him on the boat. You calmed him right down."

The door of the ER swung open for Marcus, eager to relay news. "Well, the good news is that his leg isn't broken. But his ankle is really badly sprained. He's got to stay off of it. They're doing stuff to the cut right now, cleaning it up and stitching him up," Marcus said.

"Can I go back and see him?" Damen asked, hoping to get a moment to talk to the doctor.

"Yeah, they asked that we give them a minute to get his wound cleaned out and stitched up. It's quite a process to get all the metal pieces out. It's really painful."

Damen gave the doctor a few minutes before he went in. He'd seen worse, much worse. It was a relief that Daniel's leg wasn't broken and hoped he would be back working sooner than he thought.

"How are you planning to get back to the dive site? Have you found any more help?" Marcus asked, making himself comfortable in a chair next to Lizzie. "I doubt the doctor will release him to dive for a few weeks with that cut."

Damen shook his head in frustration. "No one is interested. I can't reveal anything yet, so I've got no leverage to garner any interest."

"They'll be plenty interested once you can announce it," Marcus agreed.

"Absolutely! I just need some coverage for the next couple of weeks, but it doesn't look like I'll get it. We'll just have to work the crew we have left hard, and hope the equipment holds out."

Marcus stared at the floor for a moment as though in thought.

"You know, I am just hanging out before we have to go back to school. I'm willing and able to help if you'd have me," Lizzie offered, glancing at Marcus encouragement in her eyes.

"Oh no," Marcus replied, shaking his head. "Not me. I've had enough excitement for the next few weeks. I'm not much of a diver, anyway."

Lizzie gave him an encouraging look.

"I know, how would this work," Marcus started, "Damen, why don't you take my boat, if Lizzie will be on site my father wouldn't mind. It's being restocked right now and gassed up. Let me just call them and we'll add some groceries to the list for back-up. They'll take care of it, and it'll be ready for you when you're ready to go. You can be back on site well before daylight and beat your father out there, which I *know* you really want to do, right?"

It was a remarkably generous offer, but it came with ties. He'd have to have Lizzie be part of the crew. He wasn't sure he liked that idea, for several reasons. However, it would solve some problems, and get him back on the dive site before his father came out. He had to admit it *was* nice to have the yacht around the past few days, an extra space and working equipment made a difference.

"Are you trying to bribe him to let me be work on the wreck? Or would you like to get rid of me?" Lizzie teased Marcus.

"Oh doll, you know I'd do anything for you!" Marcus said, patting her leg. Lizzie rolled her eyes in reply. "I know you don't want to be at your parent's house."

"That's really a generous offer, but..." Damen started.

"It was my idea to go fishing. Daniel getting injured was my fault. He would have never been out if I hadn't talked him into it. I'd really like to make it up to you." Marcus interrupted. "I can take him to my house tonight, and that way your father won't catch wind of what happened until he's out on the wreck."

Damen knew Marcus was right. His father would react the same way he was about the skeleton crew, but tenfold. Marcus would know this, having been friends with Daniel since they were little kids. He knew how his father reacted.

"And I can help in Daniel's place. I'd be with experienced divers. Just give me direction. I've never done this work as you know, but I'm capable as you saw today. I won't get in the way, and I'll be productive."

Damen contemplated the proposal, pacing the waiting room's tiled floor as he mulled it over. This wasn't a terrible solution. Marcus's offer was extraordinary: the benefits of wealth. Lizzie should be able to handle the work. She was a natural diver, but she'd need guidance. Damen admitted to himself that it was exciting to have a reason to get to know her better, to understand what was drawing him in.

A functioning boat would make things so much less worrisome, they could work through equipment failures, but they needed to feed the crew if the food storage quit again, they would have a mutiny. It had been an immense help over the past few days as it was, even though he was reluctant to admit it.

His thoughts moved to Marcus. And how nice it would be to have enough money to hand over your yacht for a couple of weeks after filling it with groceries and fuel to make up for an accident that wasn't really your fault. Marcus and Lizzie lived in a world that he did not. His money, for what it was, came from his own hard work and not from his family.

"It's not a bad plan. It could work, if you're sure you want to do that." Damen replied. "Thank you!"

"Great, let me call the dock." Marcus stepped away to use his phone.

Lizzie leaned forward eagerly, her face beaming. "This will work out fine, truly. I can pull my weight. You won't have to worry."

Damen stopped his pacing to look into her face. "I'm agreeing to it. But you have to promise me you'll follow instructions, and no heroics like you tried today. That shark could have had you in its mouth...."

Lizzie swallowed hard. "Yeah, I realize that now. But I promise, nothing like that." She reached her hand out to him and he took her small hand in his, shaking in agreement. A jolt of electricity snapped between them. From her reaction, he saw she felt it too, making him wonder if this entire plan was really a bad idea.

Damen pushed aside his doubts as a deputy sheriff in uniform appeared at the door of the waiting room, his eyes scanning the occupants. Spotting Lizzie, he approached, interrupting any further exchange between them.

The deputy wasn't someone he recognized; he knew a lot of the law enforcement in the area. This guy was younger than himself, more likely around Daniel's age. Damen felt he should know him, but couldn't place him. The younger man's name badge was unreadable, as he was too far away.

Lizzie greeted him warmly, as though he were a long-time friend. "Lizzie, so good to see you. I've actually been trying to reach you. I saw Daniel was being brought in and I hoped I could catch you."

Marcus looked over from his phone call, his face full of concern with the approach of the deputy. He watched their exchange closely as he finished the call, returning quickly to his cousin's side. "Can we talk privately?" the young deputy asked her.

"It's okay," Lizzie replied, gesturing for him to take the chair next to her, the deputy eyeballed Damen suspiciously.

"What is it?" Lizzie asked, her voice urgent.

"There's been a development. I've been trying to get in touch with you for the past couple of days before the sheriff talks to your folks. I wanted to make sure that you heard about this first." The young deputy swallowed, once again giving Damen the side-eye. "They've been doing some re-furbishment at the Fort, doing some digging along the walls. Well, they found some items, including a bathing suit buried that fits the description of your sister's, that she was wearing the day she disappeared."

He hesitated as Lizzie took in a sharp breath. Marcus took the chair next to her and wrapped his arm around her shoulders.

"We're going to see if there was any DNA on the bathing suit itself. It's been buried for a long time and is not in great shape. I know there has been nothing substantial found in her case in years. If it's hers, it will be a tremendous revelation."

"Did... did they find anything else?" Marcus asks. "They combed the area pretty well a bunch of times over the years. I'm kind of surprised they didn't find this sooner."

The deputy stared blankly at Marcus before answering, understanding the deeper meaning of the question after a moment. "Ahh, right, well, there weren't any remains recovered. The sheriff has the area secured, and depending on what they find on the suit, may order more searches of the area."

Lizzie blanched, and Damen had the sudden urge to punch the guy. Where was his sensitivity?

"How long will the results take?" Lizzie asked, her voice soft as she recovered from the deputy's forthrightness.

"A couple of weeks at best," he answered. "The testing will identify any DNA on the suit."

This would be a substantial find, but finding blood or semen on Cami's suit would mean that she had been raped or killed or both. Lizzie nodded solemnly. "Let's not reveal this to my parents or anyone else until they have the results. There is no need to take them through that hell until we know something for certain."

Admiration rose in Damen's mind for Lizzie's protection of her parents. She was taking the emotional hits for them. The young deputy nodded in agreement. "You know I can't control what the sheriff does, ultimately. But he's been sensitive to the situation, knowing your parents. He won't reveal anything until he has the complete picture, if there is one." He stood, his hat in his hand.

Lizzie stood to say goodbye. "Thank you."

"And you'll be sure," he said hesitantly, gesturing to the men, "that this stays between us?"

"Of course," she said, walking him to the door of the waiting room.

Damen couldn't hear the rest of the conversation but noted the younger man was enamored with Lizzie. They briefly embraced, and he kissed her cheek before he left. She smiled wanly and waved goodbye to him.

This was definitely interesting information about her sister. He knew that no actual evidence of what happened to her had ever appeared. It was one of the great mysteries of the island, and very sad for her family. There had been plenty of theories over time about what may have transpired. Initially, the entire community had searched for her, the police overturning every stone to find any information. He recalled that also included questioning any young man who knew her on the island, including himself. An uncomfortable situation to go through, especially for someone on the other side of the tracks from the missing girl's family.

Something bothered him about the exchange between Lizzie and the deputy. The way she responded to his obvious attraction and how he looked at her. Was she interested in the guy? The guy was definitely into her. But she had a boyfriend, *his brother! Was she cheating on him?*

A slew of other questions grew in his thoughts. Why would she be so willing to leave Daniel's side to dive with him when he needed her now? Why would she want to go out on the dive site for a couple of weeks when Daniel couldn't? What kind of girlfriend was she that she wasn't willing to be with him when the chips were down? Granted, Daniel would have Marcus waiting on him, but it wouldn't be like his girl taking care of him. Doubts of her commitment to Daniel rose in his mind.

On the other hand, she was willing to meet Daniel's obligations by taking his place on the dive crew. Didn't she have other things to do, friends to hang out with? Surely, she could make better plans.

Damen stopped himself from going down that road, realizing that he shouldn't lie to himself. He was glad for his own sake that she was willing to fill in for Daniel, and particularly happy that somebody with her looks would work side by side with him for the next few weeks. It certainly would make it a little more pleasant with all the hard work and drudgery they faced. He was on leave, after all.

Overall, she seems like a decent girl, protective of her parents and one that wouldn't complain and whine about the work. It would only be for a short period. He hoped he was right, and this worked out.

Damen looked over at Lizzie, sitting with her long legs crossed in front of him, as she whispered with Marcus, their heads together.

He was attracted to her; and knew it was wrong and especially bad if they'd be working and living in close quarters. Damen *was* the family black sheep, not the favorite son, and everything he did was wrong anyway, so what would be the point of stopping now?

An image of Lizzie holding Daniel's head in her lap rose in his mind. There was no way he would purposefully hurt his brother. He swallowed deeply. *Maybe this was a bad idea.*

CHAPTER 5

A few hours later, Lizzie found herself aboard her uncle's small yacht with Damen piloting back to the dive site. They were in the flybridge in the open air; the wind felt luxurious after being in the cramped hospital waiting room for so long. Even though the air was still humid, the breeze felt great on her skin. The sky was beautiful with the sun just about to set, throwing colors of pink, red and gold along the western sky. As they skimmed over the top of the calm water, it was like glass.

Damen was busily tinkering with all the controls like a kid in a candy shop, enamored with all the electronic bells and whistles the yacht offered. Their speed was much less than when they were coming ashore, the pace calmer. Lizzie relaxed her shoulders, feeling the tension easing, the anxiety of the past few hours slipping from her muscles.

Her thoughts drifted to consider the information Paul had shared through his access as a sheriff's deputy. If the bathing suit was her sister's it opened the reality that a lot of terrible things could have happened to her. Even though these were always a possibility, there had never been any evidence that showed what had happened. Having proof that the event took place made it more tangible, and all the emotions came back with it. She was glad to know this ahead of her parents, in case it was nothing. They didn't need to go through what she was feeling now. Their response would be that much worse. Lizzie could save them that, at least.

The beach and the fort were open to anyone and regularly had visitors from all around the world. In the brief time she was alone at the beach that morning, she could have been abducted and murdered. A lot could have happened in that span of time, from where she went missing to when they realized something was wrong. They lived in paradise, horrendous events didn't happen there, especially to one of their own. It had been inconceivable.

Lizzie remembered the day she went missing and the last time she had seen her, slamming her car door and stalking off in a huff, mad at their mother. Cami was as wild as she was beautiful. How Lizzie had wanted to be like her and have her be a real sister to her, as she saw the sisters of her friends be to them. Sharing their secrets, and going places together, as only sisters could. Cami hadn't wanted to be a lifeguard, but she had tried to align her life to the path their parents wanted her to take, to get her life back on a path with a future.

And then she was gone.

Unraveling what had occurred to her became the passion of Lizzie's life. It was the only thing she could do, otherwise she was powerless. Searching made it easier for her to cope. Both of her parents had left the investigation to the police and had warned her off taking any further steps on her own. It had become an obsession for her in high school. Lizzie had few resources of her own to pursue more without her parents knowing, at least at this point in her life.

Luckily, the relationship with Paul Nichols as a part-time deputy had come in handy. He could give her inside information. Being able to have some influence over the information that was fed to her parents or prepping them on what they may learn helped her to cope. Their marriage was crumbling as it was, leading them in a false direction, would add fuel to that fire. Giving them pieces of information without conclusion or a solid lead just brought up the old pain again, gutting them time and time again.

Lizzie knew Paul had a crush on her, but he was an insider and could access information she couldn't. It was no cost to her, except for an occasional drink or meal, which made her feel like she was leading him on. It was cheap of her, she knew, to lead him on, but she would do it to get information. Someday, she vowed to use her own resources to pursue answers, hire a private investigator to solve the case. There were organizations other victim's families had founded to help support the search for their missing loved ones. She planned to do just that for Cami when she was out from under the control of her parents.

Damen spoke, cutting through her thoughts. "I'm sorry. I didn't mean to scare you. You're staring at me and I'm not sure what to think." He smiled widely, clearly in his element on the water. "Are you having second thoughts? Now you're not sure about joining me on the dive?"

His words brought her back to what they were doing on the boat and why she was here alone with this man who'd volunteered to search for Cami all those years ago. "No, sorry for you. That's not what I was thinking about. I guess I'm a million miles away."

She tried to shake off the thoughts careening around her mind and focus on what Damen was saying. He engaged the autopilot. No other boats were in sight at the moment. At this rate, the trip will take them a couple of hours to arrive at the dive site. "Thinking about what the deputy had to say?"

He sat on the bench next to her, looking out over the water and the sunset. Both were native to the area and used to the beauty of the sun and the sea. But it was still gorgeous, Lizzie thought, trying to enjoy it. "All the years of searching for Cami and trying to find out what happened to her. Now, finding a clue is a little overwhelming. There's been nothing for years, not a hair, not a fingerprint, and now this. It just brings it all back."

Damen reached out and placed his hand over her's on the bench, his touch warm and comforting. They sat in silent companionship for a few minutes, both deep in their thoughts.

"Do you still want to be on the dive?" he asked hesitantly. "We can turn around now, if you'd rather. I can bring you home."

Lizzie knew this was a meaningful gesture. They were desperate for divers to work on the wreck and losing her now would be a burden to the rest of the crew, not to mention the loss of the working yacht. His concern warmed her. She looked up into his face and smiled, tilting her head in order to look into his eyes. His eyes give away his surprise with the connection, but he held her gaze. "That's really very kind of you to offer," she said.

Damen retrieved his hand from hers and stood, moving away to busy himself with the controls again. "They won't have results for a few weeks, but I'm hopeful they'll have something to go on by the time I'm ready to leave to go back to school."

"You know I was part of the search for her.... when she first disappeared," he said. "Its surprising that there's been no evidence all this time."

Lizzie smiled at him. It was obvious he didn't remember. "Yes, I know. You took me home from the beach that day."

Taking the bench seat opposite her, Damen crossed his arms and stretched out his muscular legs. She assumed the choice of seat was to better monitor the controls, and to look around the horizon, ensuring that their course was clear of other boats. "Oh yeah! I remember that!" he laughed, "You blew your nose in my shirt!"

They both laughed. Lizzie feeling the color rise in her cheeks. It stung that he didn't remember that act of kindness without her prompting. Binging her back home that day when she was so upset had been very kind. It had stayed with her for years. In fact, she still had his now very worn t-shirt, as a staple in her nightwear. "They've found nothing substantial to go on in her case that I know of. It's almost as if she disappeared off the face of the earth."

Damen shifted his relaxed pose and leaned toward her, elbows on his knees, his hands clasped. "This is truly the first big piece of evidence if it's hers and not someone else's," Lizzie said.

He nodded in agreement. "It's kind of hard to believe that a bathing suit would survive for as long as it has buried on the beach and have any kind of DNA still intact."

"I know, but it's possible to find DNA even on remains of cave dwellers after thousands of years," she smiled at him.

"Really? Sounds like you've done some research!"

"I'm quite the amateur sleuth with a fountain of insight into forensics, all self-taught. I could teach you a thing or two!"

Their eyes connected as they laughed together, with Damen breaking the connection by leaping to his feet to study the controls, ensuring they were still on course. It seemed the boat enthralled him.

"I'd do anything to help find what happened to her. If she's still alive somewhere, or if she's..."

Damen nodded at her in understanding. Lizzie knew he didn't know what else to say. Most people reacted that way when she talked about Cami. What else can you say when the worst thing in the world has happened, and there's no answer? What can you possibly say to make it any better?

They both returned to their thoughts, the conversation lapsing as they took in the view. The sun would set soon, and they'd come onto the dive site under dark. Lizzie had all the confidence that they'd have no trouble with Damen piloting them in. There may even be some moonlight to illuminate their way.

"Can I ask you something?" Damen asked, looking over the horizon. "I was kind of curious that you would leave Daniel behind. You know, with his injury and all."

His question didn't really surprise her. She knew she'd have to tread carefully not to raise suspicions regarding her two best friends. They would reveal themselves to their families in their own time, not hers. She understood what Damen was getting at, about her willingness to be out on the dive site. Daniel was well taken care of, with Marcus staying behind. However, as his fake girlfriend, it would have behooved her to have stayed behind with him. Honestly, Lizzie couldn't face the silence of her parents' house for another few weeks before school started. And this seemed like a once in a lifetime adventure that would be a great distraction from the boredom of her life. And the worry and concern over what the police may have found. "Oh dear, you're thinking that I'm a bad girlfriend?" she replied, looking at him half accusingly.

Damen didn't answer.

"I guess I am. He'll be fine. He's well taken care of. And honestly, I'm not the best person to be caring for him. Marcus has more of a maternal and caring characteristic than I do."

Damen laughed. "Well, at least he knows where you stand."

They laughed together for a few moments, making her feel more at ease. Damen held her gaze, his expression changing to seriousness.

"You know I won't lie to you. I think that you're not the best choice to be out on the dive. But you're the best choice that I have at this moment."

He moved to take the seat next to her again. "I hope you'll not make me regret my decision to have you on the dive site. So please make sure that you do what I ask, that you follow my instructions. It'll be best that you continue to be paired with me so that I can make sure you're safe, as well as make sure that you're handling things correctly."

"We've already had this conversation, I promise." Frustration entered her voice, the tension again building in her shoulders again. *Here we go, the beast is appearing.*

He exhaled. "We have, but there's a little more to this than you may realize. Be sure to follow my guidance instead of anybody else who may feel attracted to you and may try to hit on you. Being the one woman on the crew, you're a temptation. Those men have been out there at sea for several weeks and often away from their girlfriends, or any opportunity for any sex for months at a time. They're kind of a rough bunch. I wouldn't expect any political correctness and you'll have to stand up for yourself. Try to not flirt unless you mean it."

"There's another woman on the crew..." Lizzie replied, wanting to roll her eyes, but she restrained herself.

Damen laughed, his tone sarcastic. "She's part of the crew and may be attracted to you as well."

Lizzie's stomach sank at Damen's words. They were a rough bunch, but they all seemed so nice after they'd found the treasure and were calling her their lucky charm. Maybe this was a mistake, but it wouldn't be her first time emerging herself into a chauvinist environment. Some of her pre-med courses and labs were filled with the same sort, not as rough and tumble as the crew, but male sexists through and through. She could handle herself, and since Damen would pair with her and she would sleep on the yacht, there'd be less interaction. She could do anything for a couple of weeks. They had all seemed genuine enough, and hardworking.

"The other concern is security. It may be a few days before we get any security out on the site. We'll need one or two guys, anyway. Not divers, we'll need them fully engaged in the recovery. Once the word gets out, we've found this treasure, we could be in danger of others wanting to get a piece of the pie."

Lizzie thought about staying alone on her uncle's boat at night. Would she be in danger? Not that she was concerned about the crew; she could handle herself and didn't expect any sinister behavior from them. They'd all been loyal to the Wisler business through the tough times and would certainly stick with them now they'd hit the motherlode. It was the talk of security for the treasure itself that concerned her. Visions of modern-day pirates rose in her mind. "Am I going to be okay sleeping alone on the boat?"

Damen clenched his jaw, his knuckles becoming white underneath his skin. "I hadn't thought of that," he said. Clearly, her presence caused another wrinkle for him to deal with. "I doubt Sally would make much of a pleasant companion and it's pretty darn nice accommodations... I'd be more comfortable keeping an eye on you myself, for Daniel's sake. I'll stay on the yacht with you. If that's okay. I can take Daniel's bunk."

Immediately Lizzie panicked. Daniel and Marcus had been staying together in the master suite while she'd been on the smaller side where there were two separate berths, each with its own bathroom and shower. "Daniel has been staying with me," she lied. "I'm sure Marcus wouldn't want anyone to stay in his suite. He has some particularities about his things. There's another bunk and private bath for you or whoever you'd like to stay on the boat with me. And of course, the deck and the salon area are also places where people can crash if they'd like. I actually spend most nights up on deck... I'm a little claustrophobic."

Damen stared at her, contemplating, his fingers stroking the stubble on his chin, his expression unreadable. "Okay then," Damen agreed. "I'll stay here tonight, and we'll work things out in the morning. You really shouldn't be staying on the boat by yourself. It'd be easy to slip aboard and take you hostage for a piece of the treasure."

A shiver raced up her spine. Surely that kind of scenario was highly unlikely. Damen's concern was likely influenced by his work in the US special forces. There would be an element of danger, but she was certain her response was more related to the fact that they would stay alone on the yacht together.

CHAPTER 6

Damen climbed up the dive ladder from the relatively cool water of the Gulf and stepped into the steamy air on the rusty deck of the *Merchant*. His arm muscles aching as he pulled himself onto the deck and slipped off his flippers, dropping his weight belt with a heavy clank. A breeze blew off the water, reducing the heavy humidity of the South Florida summer. Damen removed his tanks before turning to help Lizzie with the bucket. Working as a team, they carried the heavy load to the surface from their work this morning. They had loaded it with coins and items melded with coral and sea life. Damen pulled the bucket towards him as he lifted, his back and neck muscles straining, while Lizzie pushed from below, finally landing on the deck.

Immediately, Pierre, the marine archeologist, made his way over to the pair to see what they'd pulled up. "Look here, Pierre," Lizzie said, pulling a small encrusted box from the bucket. "This looks like a jewelry box. "

Pierre studied the box carefully as Lizzie slid her fingers along the lid, opening the muck lined box, her fingers searching to see if there was an object inside. Immediately, a smile of wonder filled her face as she lifted a perfectly preserved gold and emerald cross.

Pierre and Lizzie put their heads together, admiring the find, chattering away. The archeologist's excitement was palpable, even though he was a typical staunch and quiet scientist. His presence has been actually very helpful during this trip, creating a refined process for his work. Lizzie had taken to asking him endless questions, fascinated with the history of the objects they found.

Damen had expected lengthy delays for Pierre to log and photograph everything. But having him on board had not hindered their retrieval of the objects at the bottom of the ocean. And they'd been able to catalog and collect a lot of information and data about the overall wreck itself.

His father stood on the deck, high and dry, with his flowered Aloha shirt, sunglasses and Panama hat. He looked like a mob boss observing the expanse of his empire flanked by armed guards. Damen had positioned visible security on the fly deck of the *Merchant* and over on the yacht, continuously scanning the horizon for any other boats that may come into the area interested in their discovery. There were literally millions and millions of dollars already stored in the hull of the *Merchant,* on the yacht, and still scattered over the seabed floor.

Pierre Smith had identified the wreck as being that of the *Atocha* lost centuries ago, never found by another human being until he and Lizzie found it just days ago. It was a little heady to be the first people in centuries to have touched the items the dive team was bringing up. This was what drove treasure hunters like his father and Damen understood it, having been swept up in it with their find on this wreck.

"Let me see what you got there," Isaac called to Lizzie and Pierre, their heads still together, chatting over the morning haul.

Lizzie turned out to be a great help and a hard worker. So far, she'd kept her word about following his instructions.

Her work ethic had been a tremendous benefit to the overall team. The dive team and the rest of the crew continued to refer to her as their 'lucky charm'. They hadn't had any further accidents or equipment breaking down since that last disastrous day when they found the *Atocha*, and all the cob jobs they'd concocted were holding. They'd been very lucky with the finds from the bottom of the ocean. It was unbelievable what they were bringing up, and what was still down there. It could be one of the top treasures in the world.

Damen grew more intrigued by Lizzie with each passing day. Even though she was his little brother's girlfriend, he found himself drawn to her and admired her willingness to work so hard. There was a lot more going on under the surface of this college girl. There was a depth that drew him in and made him want to explore further.

At night, he heard her footsteps above his head, pacing the deck, likely consumed with thoughts about what the police had found in her sister's case. Most mornings, he'd found her sleeping on the deck chair. It made him wonder how long she'd been this restless, or if it was because of the new information.

Damen was no stranger to stress impacting his sleep. He'd lost countless hours after missions that had gone sideways, especially this last one. He pushed the memory from his mind; it had been better since taking leave. The crushing anxiety and nightmares had eased. Even though the work on the dive site was hard, he was enjoying it, mostly because of Lizzie's easy companionship. They'd established a rhythm in their work. She was a natural diver and not afraid of hard labor, considering her background. Their evenings comprised eating together and a game of cards or working on a jigsaw puzzle she'd produced from one of the many storage compartments on the yacht. A few nights he'd joined the crew on the *Merchant* for a game of poker. It wasn't the vacation most people would want, but it was doing the trick for him.

Finding the treasure had made the trip and work even more worthwhile, having taken part in the search on and off for the past years while working for his father. It was joyous to be pulling up gold and silver, after all this time. They would all get a share of the treasure after the expected lengthy processes of appraisals and legal battles they'd experienced with the other treasures in the years past. His own share would be substantial. It made him glad for the long awaited success for his father's company. At least he'd be leaving the old man with something to show for all his work. It reduced the guilt he felt by not accepting his father's legacy of the salvage business as his own.

Overall, they'd satisfied Isaac with the operation. Damen was glad he'd come out to see their overall success over the past few days. He knew deep down that he still wanted his father's approval. Isaac had even been willing to put resources into what was needed to make the dive even more successful. Mechanics had tended the equipment and were are available to travel out to fix anything that would break in the future. A team just finished working on the bilge pumps that had been a constant plague. They needed to be replaced, which would mean a few days out of service for the ship. Damen had lost count of the jerry-rigs they'd done to avoid capsizing the piece of floating junk. He needed to encourage his father to plan to get them replaced sooner rather than later.

Isaac lifted the gold cross out in front of him, admiring its surprising beauty. Its gold glinted in the morning sun. The cross was a carefully crafted piece. Its delicate chain spoke to the status of its owners. "It's absolutely beautiful," Lizzie said. "I can't believe how shiny it is after being underneath the ocean for hundreds of years. Look at it. It's just perfect."

"Gold doesn't tarnish in sea water. It doesn't harm the material," Pierre offered, his tone patiently instructive.

"Look at that handiwork!" Isaac exclaimed, running the delicate chain through his fingers. "You know, there was Cuban aristocracy lost in this wreck. Heading back to the motherland."

Isaac ran his fingers over the green emeralds, contemplating. "You know your mother hasn't held me in the highest regard since she found out we were searching for the *Atocha* years ago. She told me I was a grave robber, digging in the graves of her ancestors, pillaging sacred areas that should remain undisturbed. That we should leave them as they were hundreds of years ago. Lost at sea with the hurricane. You may not know this, my dear Lizzie, but we used to be friends. Your mother and I, a long time ago. Maybe this will mend her feelings toward me."

He slipped the necklace over a stunned Lizzie's head. A breeze swirled up around them, blowing Isaac's Panama hat off his head, dangerously near the dive deck, close to the water's edge. Pierre scurried to retrieve it for him before it went into the water.

A tingle raced down Damen's spine as the warm breeze ruffled his hair dry from his morning dive. He felt his senses go on alert, as they did on a mission when he knew the enemy was near. He brushed the feeling off.

Lizzie's fingers touched the cross at her neck, speechless. "We'll have to catalog it and sort through all the accounting for it. But I'd like for you to have it, as payment for helping us out on the dive. Everyone who is part of the discovery and salvage will get a portion of the treasure. This will be part of yours."

Her eyes widened. "I... I... didn't realize that..." she said, stumbling over her words.

Isaac patted her shoulder. "I'd like you to show your mother, let her know. I don't know if it would change her feelings toward me, but I'd feel better about it." Isaac interrupted, taking Lizzie's hand tightly in his. "Let her know."

With that, Isaac dropped Lizzie's hand and headed to the bridge, expecting Damen to follow. Lizzie trailed behind the archeologist, fingering the cross around her neck, a puzzled look on her face. Isaac had that effect on people. It was his way of dropping a lot of information on you and then exiting, leaving more questions than answers in his wake.

Damen considered his father's action. It was out of character for him to just *give away* a piece of treasure before he even knew its value. The necklace would be valuable, for certain, likely much more than the value of Lizzie's labors for the past few days. Damen shook his head. When he was a little boy, he recalled Lizzie's mother, Soledad, being around. She'd been friendly with his father. The memories were vague and disconnected, as he had been so young. Isaac's action today made Damen wonder the true nature of their relationship. It had been long before Lizzie or her sister were born.

Damen joined his father on the bridge overlooking the operation below. Isaac reached up to pat his son on the shoulder, a rare gesture of affection for the gruff man. "Still planning on heading back to the service? Wouldn't you want to have a life like this? Finding treasure? Instead of working as a sailor for the rest of your life?"

Damen sighed, his father's generous mood slipping away as the two men slid back into their old discussion. His father wanted him to take over the family business. He was getting older and wanted to have a plan for one of his sons to step into his shoes. He'd grown tired of the overall day in day out grind of trying to finance treasure hunts and grapple with the federal and state governments. But had been his dream, not Damen's.

Finding the gold, finding the treasure, and the overall hunt has been his passion. Damen had just been along for the ride for most of his life. Although finding this treasure made the possibility of it appealing, it wasn't what Damen wanted in life. His life was in the SEALs, it was part of him now.

The full recovery of the *Atocha* would take a couple of years to gather everything from the wreck and to preserve as much as they could. Isaac had aspirations of bringing the entire hull and other items into his museum in Key West. Damen just did not see himself as part of that.

"I haven't changed my mind," Damen replied. "But I'd like a couple of days back in port to do some errands, see some old friends and take a few days before I head back."

Isaac stroked his short beard. "Your brother's coming along pretty well. I think I can send him out to relieve you. I know he's got to pull things together to go back to school. He can do that now, or Lizzie can do it for him when she goes back. He'll give you a reprieve at the end of the week."

Damned nodded in agreement, glad Daniel was healing well enough to consider being out on the wreck site. "Any luck getting more help?"

"I've got a few men interested. Word's out that we've made this find. More salvagers are cropping up everywhere. I should have my pick. The man I want, and trust if you aren't going to be here, will be available in a few days."

Damen nodded, glad that his father had found more help that he had confidence in. "Will you have a diver to replace Lizzie and Andy? Have you heard if he'll be back?"

He hadn't had the chance to check in on the injured Andy, but knew his father would have. "He's still banned from diving for a few more weeks. I'll bring him back when he's ready. He's a hard worker and has hung in with me. That Lizzie has been pulling her weight, it seems, she hasn't been a bad replacement for your brother. I have to say she surprised me, being willing to jump in like she has."

"Yeah, she's been a great help. The crew likes her."

"She's easy on the eyes," Isaac replied, looking at him slyly.

Damen had always hated his father's treatment of women, always looking at them as though they were possessions, and not intelligent beings. That he was looking at his son's girlfriend in that light was downright creepy, although he'd had a girlfriend or two around Lizzie's age. It didn't make it right. His response to his father surprised himself. If he was being honest with himself, *he* didn't like him thinking of her in that light. He shook it off; she wasn't his girl. He'd no right to think of her in that way.

"She'll be done with us at the same time as me," Damen replied with a little more attitude in his voice than necessary. Isaac didn't comment if he noticed it, thankfully. He didn't need his father questioning his feelings for the girl.

"No problem. We'll get the *Viking* out here with the new crew set up by the end of the week. Get this hunk of junk fixed up. You and Lizzie can take *that* with you." He pointed at the yacht and turned away from Damen, the conversation over.

Damen watched Isaac take off in his boat while lighting a cigar, the mechanics and workers staggering around the deck at the rapid acceleration of the engines. A few days ago, Isaac was struggling to find money to make the payroll and today he was a rich man. This was the stuff Isaac lived for. Although not part of the work crew on the dive any longer, he was eager to hear the progress and see the treasures as they arrived at port.

Damen wondered if his father would put pressure on Daniel now he'd made it clear he wasn't interested in the business. He doubted Daniel would step in and hoped he'd finish his education and find his own way. Daniel had a bright future, and a great girlfriend. His thoughts drifted back to his father's comments about Lizzie. He couldn't hide from it. Lizzie had been really pleasant to be around, even working as hard as they did. Neither had seemed to mind their close quarters. They got along well. He knew he'd miss her company once the job was over.

He'd found her sitting quietly occasionally, looking out over the water, making him wonder what she was thinking. She was the first women in a long time whose thoughts intrigued him. He knew he couldn't hide from himself, he was attracted to her. Something he hadn't acted on, but he'd thought about it. He wanted to delve into her thoughts and then run his hands along the length of her firm body.

He shook it off, knowing he couldn't take any steps towards that end because she was Daniel's girl. His brother came first. Brotherly love was more important than the guilt he would face if he allowed himself to pursue his desires. Thankfully, she hadn't shown the same level of attraction to him; instead, she'd been friendly and kind. He didn't know if his resolve would hold if she were to make a move in his direction. They had only days left together, so he wasn't likely to find out.

CHAPTER 7

Damen gently shook Lizzie's shoulder as she slept in the deck chair. "Hey, wake up! A storm is coming," he said urgently, kneeling next to her. "I need to move the boat away from the *Merchant* in order that the boats don't collide during the storm. You're going to want to come in. It's going to be pretty bad for a while."

Sleepy and disoriented in the pre-dawn light, Lizzie pulled her things together. She'd carried a few items with her last night when she couldn't sleep: a light blanket, her phone, and a picture frame. Damen sat at the boat controls, pulling the boat away from the *Merchant*. The engine roared to life with the anchor rising into the hull with a clang.

Already the boat rocked on the water, forcing her to steady herself as she studied the weather app next to Damen's pilot chair. The radar displayed a large storm heading their way. "I guess I haven't been paying attention to the weather," she said. "It looks like we're going to have a big change. Were we expecting this to happen?"

He was busy guiding the boat to a safe distance from the *Merchant*. "Yes, and no. A front is moving in and it's coming further south than what they originally predicted. We'll get a couple of days of bad weather if it hangs over us."

"Can we dive during a storm?" Lizzie asks.

The lights from the *Merchant* moved into the distance. "It really doesn't affect you underwater. But it's pretty difficult to get on and off the boat when there's bad weather and you can get hurt. We're probably not going to dive for a day or two, depending on how bad we get it."

Lizzie moved carefully to the couches, sitting back and looking out over the ocean. Lightning flashed in the distance, illuminating the sky to the north. Streaks of red and gold highlighted the impending sunrise in the eastern sky.

Damen finished tending to the boat, making sure everything was secure. Grabbing himself a coke from the refrigerator, taking a seat next to Lizzie on the couch. The lightning show drew both their attention as the storms approached, flashing across the sky with both beautiful and frightening power.

"Do you get seasick?" he asked, sipping on his coke.

Lizzie shook her head, smiling. "Haven't yet. But I can't recall being out for any length of time in a storm."

"I guess we're going to find out. Might rock like this and more for quite a while."

"Should we think about going in?"

"It'll be worse traveling in it. Key West was supposed to get the brunt of the storm. We were below the front, and it was originally supposed to miss us altogether. If it pulls back to its original track, we should have a chance for a few days of good diving before we have to leave. If you're okay with that."

That meant a couple of days confined together on the yacht. Lizzie nodded her agreement, and their gazes returned to watching the storm. "Will you go back to bed?" Damen asked. "I don't know if I can sleep anymore."

Lizzie answered him with a shrug of her shoulder.

"I noticed you don't sleep very much. It's kind of surprising considering that we've been working pretty hard. When my head hits the pillow, I'm out."

"I get to sleep okay, and then I wake up and... well... my mind races," Lizzie replied hesitantly.

"I'm sorry, it was a personal question..."

"It's fine," Lizzie said, resting her palm on his arm. "I don't mind."

The connection against his skin felt warm and solid. She kept her hand on his arm longer than was necessary, looking into his face, finding it open and kind. Their eyes connected for a moment. She felt a spark of warmth in her chest and hastily pulled her hand away.

Damen cleared his throat, taking a sip of his soda.

"I guess I have a lot to think about," Lizzie started. "Life. What comes next.... after school is done. You know, the usual stuff. Where I'm headed, where I'm going, what my life will be like when I'm done with college. What I want to do with my life."

"Medical school, right? You're pre-med?" he asked.

Lizzie sighed. "I'd like to go into law, have a legal practice doing investigations, forensics and those kinds of things. But my father is not encouraging me to do that. He wants me to be a doctor, just like him." She smiled at him. "I think you understand what I'm talking about with your father, wanting you to take over the business."

He nodded, taking a big gulp of his drink. "Yeah... I totally understand."

Damen jumped to his feet, checking the doors leading to the deck, ensuring they were sealed. After he checked the galley, making sure they'd battened the appliances and kitchen items down. "Do you want anything to drink?" he asked, opening the small refrigerator. He retrieved a bottle of water before she replied, setting it on the end table next to her.

He paused before sitting back down, his eyes drawn to the curves of her body beneath her choice of nightwear. She had a t-shirt on and boxer shorts. It wasn't the skimpy attire she wore that made her feel self-conscience, working side-by-side in her bikini or form defining wet suit for days. It was the way he was looking at her. Just for a beat, she'd seen a flash of desire in his eyes, gone as quickly as it had come. *Had she been imagining it?*

He took the seat next to her again. "Sorry, I didn't mean to stare. But I had a T-shirt just like the one you're wearing."

Her cheeks felt hot, her embarrassment palpable as she lowered her gaze. "Actually... it was yours." She shifted uncomfortably in her seat on the couch.

They sat silently for a moment. Lizzie felt she could almost hear him thinking about what she'd just said. There was no noise except for waves hitting the hull and the occasional creak of the rocking boat. After an awkward moment, Damen spoke. "Have you heard anything from the police?" Damen asked.

"No, I have heard nothing," Lizzie answered, shaking her head. "I... I'm not really sure I want to hear. It's been so long not knowing anything that I'm afraid of finding out what may have happened."

"It's hard to believe that there's been nothing all this time." Damen reached out to touch the end of her t-shirt, his shirt, his fingers brushing against her bare skin, sending a jolt of electricity up her spine. "It's pretty worn out..."

Embarrassed, Lizzie pulled the material from his fingers. "It's pretty old...."

"It's a good shirt. It was my favorite band. I saw them for the first time that summer. How long has it been now?" Damen appeared to be doing math in his head. He reached over to take the frame she had brought in with her from the deck. "This is her? I remember her. She was behind me in school."

"It's been 8 years." Lizzie replied, her voice breaking as she looked at the photo with him. "That was taken a few days before she went missing. Eight years today."

To her embarrassment, tears welled in her eyes. She turned her face away as they fell down her cheeks.

"Hey, I'm sorry. I didn't mean to upset you. I was just curious." Damen said, wrapping his arm around her shoulder.

Lizzie allowed herself to lean into him as he attempted to console her. His solid chest comforting. "It's just I wonder whatever happened to her, and what it would be like if she were alive now."

She swallowed hard as the tears welled up in her eyes and then spilled down her cheeks. Damen pulled her into his arms, so that she was half sitting on his lap, her face buried in his chest. The contact was soothing, reminiscent of eight years ago when he held her in a similar fashion.

They stayed that way as the boat rocked them. Lightening flashing outside, she was safe in his arms. Damen brushed his hands over the length of her hair. Her tears stilling at the change in their contact. She'd cried for years for her lost sister; she wasn't sure she had much of anything left.

Damen's hand moved slowly and deliberately down her back, sending a wave of warmth with each stroke as he pulled her in closer to him. As they melted into each other, the surrounding air grew warmer, and the fire in her rose. She pulled back to look into his face. Her heart fluttered at the smoldering look in his eyes, mirroring the emotions she had been struggling with for days.

With a breathless sigh, she closed the gap between them, her lips brushing his in a tantalizing dance. Their mouths met in a delicious breeze of a kiss, lips tasting, exploring, and sending a tingling sensation down to her belly.

As they broke apart, the passion between them exploded into an inferno. He pulled her closer, and she wrapped her arms around his neck, her fingers weaving through his hair. Their lips fused again, his hands roaming her body freely, setting her skin ablaze with every touch.

His lips found her neck, tracing their way to the crest of her breasts, his hands finding them bare under the old t-shirt. He shuddered as her nipples hardened in his hands.

Suddenly, he pushed her back, holding her by her shoulders, their upper bodies no longer touching. The moment shattered. "Lizzie," he said, his voice a tortured whisper, "I can't.... I can't do this.... Daniel. You're my brother's girl."

Lizzie's heart sank, the ruse for Daniel and Marcus' sake, costing her dearly.

He turned her so her back was to him, pulling her down on the couch, still wrapped in his arms. He shifted to make them comfortable, pulling her light blanket over their legs. "It's all right, now watch the storm or go to sleep," Damen commanded.

Despite the conflicting emotions that raged inside her, she felt safe and protected. Her body burned for more, but for now, she would settle for the comfort of his embrace.

CHAPTER 8

A crackling sound on the ship's radio stirred her from sleep. She felt rested, unlike most mornings when the light of day was not welcome. Her thoughts, intrusions of nightmare imagination and a desperate longing for answers disturbed most of her nights. But not last night. The muscular arms that had encircled her for the night slipped from her waist as Damen moved from their position on the couch to answer the radio's call. Immediately, Lizzie felt the cooler air surround her as the heat from his body left her skin. Heat rose to her checks, remembering their exchange in the night and her bravado in kissing him. Her fingers touched her lips. *He'd kissed her back.*

She sat up quickly, her body tensing. *What was she doing?* As Daniel's girl, fake as those it was, kissing her boyfriend's brother was not in line with the overall cover. She glanced over at Damen, his broad back to her, talking into the radio. The content of the discussion on the radio caught her immediate attention.

"Taking on water...." the voice said. The storm was still raging outside, the boat rocking in the waves. They built the power catamaran to take the seas, even so, they rocked steadily.

"It's the damn bilge pump again. Have you checked on it?" Damen replied, positioning himself so he could see the

Merchant through the rain. "You're on an even keel from where we are."

"Yeah, can you get to the pump? Let me walk you through the repair. We've done some modifications to make it function."

Lizzie turned away from Damen's conversation as he explained in detail the steps to take to repair the pump. She moved to look at the *Merchant* in the waves. There was no way she could imagine that Damen could get onto the other boat without endangering himself. Those were moves for experienced sailors or magicians.

She looked sidelong back to Damen as he continued to give instruction. He was an experienced shipman and a SEAL, according to Daniel. Momentarily, Lizzie had a scene in her mind of Damen rappelling from the yacht to the *Merchant* James' Bond style. She smiled to herself. He certainly was built for it with his muscled arms and chest. *Control yourself!* She felt the heat rise again in her face and in her lower body.

"Hey, sorry to wake you," Damen said, reaching around her to the binoculars on the window ledge. "They're taking on water with that damn malfunctioning pump. If he can't get it straighten out, I'm going to need to get over there."

The stress rolled off him as he gazed through the binoculars. "Lack of maintenance on this equipment, damn it, she's heavy with the silver bars we brought up. We could lose her."

The immediate danger struck Lizzie. She knew the bilges were there to clear out any water leaks from rough seas but had never thought much about if they failed. It was clear, however, if the pumps were to fail, the ship could sink. The bars and extra weight from the treasure they had worked so hard to bring up over the past few days made it riskier. It had been days since they last sent in a load in with the supply ship, and they had made substantial progress in their salvage efforts.

"We could end up salvaging two ships?"

Damen took the binoculars from his face and looked sternly at Lizzie. The stare making her feel like shrinking down into the cushions she kneeled on, obviously not the right thing to say in the circumstance.

Static from the radio interrupted his retort. "Got it! It's working, water's already going down."

Damen's shoulder's visibly relaxed as he answered the *Merchant's* captain. The crisis averted. The two men continued the conversation to discuss weather and further dive plans.

Lizzie busied herself in the galley kitchen, making a pot of coffee. From the conversation on the weather, it sounded like they were in for several more hours on rough seas. Plans were being made to resume the salvage in the morning, potentially even later this afternoon. Lizzie knew that safety conscious Damen was not in favor of night diving, simply because of the added risks, sharks being one of them.

"Making coffee?" Damen asked, startling her by standing behind her at the sink.

His closeness made her jumpy. Things had definitely changed between them last night with the kiss. She turned to face him, her hand subconsciously tugging the hem of her t-shirt, *his t-shirt,* over her exposed thighs. His eyes followed her hand's movement, and his gaze slowly rose from her body to her face.

Lizzie could feel the heat rise in her cheeks. "I... I can make some pancakes, if you're hungry," she stammered.

"Sounds great," Damen said, his gaze not wavering from her face.

"Let me go get dressed," she murmured, pushing past him to the steps.

She was acting like a blushing schoolgirl. Their kiss last night had awakened her long ago crush. Their interaction this morning should have been as working partners, as they had been easily functioning over the past days. It hadn't appeared to have unsettled him in the least. He likely still saw her as the pimply teen, a kid, and his little brother's girl. That she was still wearing his t-shirt, sleeping in it after all this time, would have revealed that crush.

Any relationship with him was doomed before it began as they were both had plans to leave the area. His Navy career, her educational aspirations, would keep them apart. Not to mention she was supposed to be his brother's girl. It was impossible.

Then why was she thinking about kissing him again?

Angry with herself, she slammed the door to her private head. Peeled off the suspect t-shirt and stepped into the shower, hoping the water would wash away her desire and bring her back to her senses.

CHAPTER 9

He gripped the counter, watching his knuckles turn white, hearing the door below banging and the water start for her shower. Forcing himself to breathe, just as in diving, he could gain control of his senses and release the counter from his grasp. He'd wanted to follow her down the stairs to her quarters and help her take off that old t-shirt, drag it over her smooth skin, soft under his fingers. What he wanted to do after that, he forced from his mind.

He wanted her. He wanted her desperately. After their kiss last night, he'd held her in his arms through the night, eventually settling into sleep after wrestling with his desire to turn her to face him and press himself into her soft curves. It was so tempting and so wrong.

What kind of monster was he, anyway? She'd been crying, upset over the morbid memory of the day her sister disappeared. He'd comforted her as a long-time friend and older protective brother of her boyfriend.

But she had kissed him, the memory of that soft kiss, so sweet and so so sexy. Her soft lips sliding over his, sparking the fire that burned within him. It was an invitation, a permit to act on his hidden desire. She obviously hadn't been thinking clearly.

Lizzie was his brother's girlfriend. What kind of fiend was he to be kissing her, to be wanting her when she belonged to someone else? There were rules, codes of honor between brothers. She was off limits.

It had been *she* who had kissed him! What was it that was going through her mind? Was she playing loose with him? Lizzie surely had been chummy with the deputy. Maybe she was just playing his brother along. He looked around the yacht. Maybe she was a bored and spoiled rich kid, getting her kicks in trying to have two brothers. Trying to gain the bragging rights of such a feat, share it with her friends on social media or whatever people did these days.

Damen stopped himself. Deep in his gut, he knew she was not that person, not someone that would toy with the feelings of two brothers. She was a decent, very likeable person, and very hardworking. She certainly proved herself to be industrious over the past days while they worked endlessly to bring up the *Atocha*'s treasure. Damen had to admit that she showed genuine tenderness toward Daniel when he'd been injured.

But she had also been willing to leave him to be on the dive boat when he needed help. Marcus was there as his best friend, but shouldn't a loving girlfriend be tending to him in his hour of need and disability, caring for his needs and comforting him in his pain?

Somehow, it didn't add up for him. There was something not quite right in Daniel and Lizzie's relationship that bothered him. He wasn't able to put his finger on it, keeping it just out of his reach. Unfortunately, it was offering him an opening, an opportunity to have some grown-up fun while waiting out the weather. Lizzie didn't strike him either, as someone who would willingly hop into bed with him just to pass the time. Even if she started with the first kiss, it wasn't likely in her nature. But maybe he was reading it all wrong. She was confused and vulnerable in the moment, subconsciously mixing him up with his brother.

It was an appealing idea, however. Getting her into his bed, rocking together in the waves for a few hours until they could dive again. Who would know? They would both be on their way out of town in a few days, unlikely to cross paths again.

She could end up being his sister-in-law, making holidays and family get together awkward. If his family did those things, that is.

Damen followed Lizzie's path down the steps to the berths. He needed a cold shower and to get his mind out off of what he'd like to do with her lithe body. He hoped there were enough games or some other distractions to get him through the next 24 hours.

When he was done showering, Lizzie was busy making pancakes in the galley kitchen. It smelled wondrous. She had pulled her long hair into a severe ponytail, and looked the part of a freshly scrubbed cheerleader, her cheeks flushed and eyes bright with the activity.

Damen had located a board game that would easily occupy them for hours while they waited for the storm to move on. Already the wind was calming, and the rocking of the boat was less uneven and choppy as the waves reduced in size. Diving in the morning would be definite if the weather continued calming.

The *Merchant* was faring well with the cob-job repair of the bilge pumps holding. They were out of danger of capsizing for now. He would be certain to remind his father regarding the list of repairs needed on the old tin can. Damen shook his head. It really was crazy how they patched the equipment together. They were on their last legs financially before they had found the *Atocha*. It would be a game of catch-up with the repairs. He'd make sure his father continued to spend the money to ensure things were in good working order. It would be just like the old man to hold off on maintenance, to enhance the company's profit, even if to just re-assure the investors, rather than fatten his own pockets.

He watched Lizzie as she scooted around the small kitchen. The crew had dubbed her their lucky charm. Maybe she was. Beads of perspiration glistened on her brow as she placed a pile of delicious smelling pancakes in front of him. He smiled up at her, and she blushed immediately. The pink of her cheeks deepening as he watched her retreat a few steps away, busying herself with the plates of food.

It was obvious the attraction between them was mutual. He pushed down the flutter that rose in his belly. *A few more hours to go! Just hold it together.*

They ate heartily in compatible silence; he was ravenous for the food. Damen could hardly speak his thanks for her cooking efforts, mumbling his thanks between forkfuls of blissful buttery goodness. A guilt washed over him as he thought of the crew in the *Merchant*, likely having cold sand-wiches for their meal. He held the sentiment briefly. While he was eating well, he was in a war with himself to not leap over the table and take Lizzie in his arms. He definitely would rather be here, he thought to himself.

Shortly, he pushed the plate away, full and content. "Thanks for cooking. I didn't mean for you to wait on me. It was delicious."

They both rose simultaneously to gather the dishes, the color returning to her cheeks again. "Here, let me. I'll pick up," Damen said, taking her dish from her hands. "It's only fair, you cook. I eat and clean up."

Lizzie stood awkwardly, wiping her hands on her hips. "Yeah, all right, everything is right there."

"I can handle it. I know my way around KP."

She moved to the farthest point away from him. It limited the choices of where to be on the boat with the weather. She could retreat to her cabin, and she appeared to be considering it. He wanted her to stay on deck. "Do you want to play a game? Help to pass the time?" he asked, gesturing to the one he'd located earlier.

"Oh yes," she answered, her tone shifting. "Let's play cards. Do you like to play Gin Rummy?"

Damen watched intrigued as Lizzie gathered a deck of cards and expertly shuffled. It was definitely not her first time with cards in her hands. She handled them like a Vegas dealer. "Maybe, if you're up for it, that is. We could play for money, make it more interesting?" she asked, raising one brow, dealing the cards expertly on the table.

He laughed out loud. "Sounds intriguing. It also sounds like I'm in trouble."

CHAPTER 10

The card games were what they needed to bring them back into their usual friendly working routine. The kiss from last night was still on her mind. There was no way she could push it from her memory. It had happened. She'd been the instigator.

So far, she was winning with Damen, indebted to her by several dollars. He'd already checked in a few times with the *Merchant* to make sure the bilge pumps continued to run and to check on weather reports, collaborating on dive plans for the morning.

It had been a relief that they could return to their usual camaraderie. This morning had been tense. Damen kept looking at her as though he wanted to eat her. It was disconcerting. He likely thought poorly of her and her disregard for her relationship with Daniel. Little did he know, however, what the full truth of the matter was. She'd placed Damen in a difficult position, pitting brother against brother for her affection. The reality wasn't that, but he didn't know the actual story. She knew she needed to address it with him to clear the air. She needed him to understand that she wasn't a bad person, even if it removed any further possibility of him touching her again.

Someday, when Daniel was ready to tell his family of his true nature, she would be vindicated. But now the man sitting across from her surely had other ideas. None of them placed her in a good light. They needed to talk about it and clear the air. She was reluctant to do so right now, however, as they had just regained their easy relationship. It would be a shame to end it now, particularly with the limited time they had left together.

They would dive another two days and then they would head into Key West. It would be the end of her salvage diving career. She needed to prepare to return to school and catch up with the deputy to see what the investigation had revealed. Damen needed to get back to whatever he was heading into.

Two days left.

A feeling of despair and emptiness filled her belly. She wanted more time with him, wanted him to see who she really was. She wanted to feel the way she felt when he touched her; it made her head spin. It wasn't possible without revealing Daniel's secret, one she had vowed to keep quiet from his family. To continue the charade would also mean that reasonably anything further with Damen would be out of the question. It felt like she would lose more than just the two days they had left working on the salvage crew.

The discussion on the radio caught her attention. Hurricane? "What are they saying the path might be?" Damen asked. He spoke into the radio, flipping through the apps in the control panel.

Lizzie rose from the table to help Damen locate the weather and radar controls. A few clicks on the high-tech navigation system showed a formation far off the African coast. It had to be days to weeks out from any kind of impact on the Gulf or the Caribbean, but it was still being reported because of the favorable conditions for the system to intensify.

There had already been storm predictions a few times already this season, with the tropical storms turning a path to the north and out to sea before they affected their area. Early reporting had its benefits, allowing early preparation. More often than not, at this early stage, the track of the storm was not predictable. Preparing for storms that would never reach you took away the concern of many in the area. Making the warnings slip into the noise of the news, while giving ample notice to prepare and move out of its way once it developed and its path was definite.

Lizzie thought of the wreck beneath them. The passengers of the *Atocha* had had no warning. Their lives were in peril the moment they left the harbor in Cuba, laden with the gold and silver they salvaged now from the deep. Treasure whose weight likely helped to sink them faster once they took on water. The hurricane that killed them and so many others had no way of being forecasted and they had set sail regardless of the danger they faced.

The timing of the storm would matter to the salvage operations. They would likely need to be suspended for time. Damen signed off the radio and they both silently watched the weather report standing closely together.

"Looks like it may be bad, if it really comes this way," Lizzie said.

"Yeah, it bears watching. It could turn either way. Look at the path prediction models. It's all over the place. They don't really know right now what it will do yet, but there's a big difference between Cuba and South Carolina for a track. But the conditions are favorable. The warm water will fuel a storm this time of the year," Damen replied.

"Will they stop the salvage altogether?"

Damen looked out at the churning water between the yacht and the *Merchant* where orange buoys floated in the waves marking the wreck below. "Knowing my father, they'll stay out until the last minute to get back safely. If it's really bad, it could further spread the wreck over the bottom. Just like it had been when it first went down. That's why she's been so hard to locate. Hurricanes dragged her from her original wreck site. It could really disrupt the entire process of recovery."

"We only have a couple more days before we head in. Hopefully, things turn. I've got some things to do before we head back to school."

"According to my father, you'll be prepping for the both of you. Daniel will be on the *Viking* until the day you go back up north. He'd keep him here indefinitely if he could. He'd like you both, all hands, you know."

"I'm sure," she answered, trying to not have a perturbed tone. Isaac's authoritarian attitude toward her toward her role in getting his son ready to go back to college savored of chauvinism. Little did he know Marcus was their coordinator, of all things domestic. Their two-bedroom apartment was tastefully decorated and well stocked, thanks to him. She only had to consider her own needs, which were few and centered on her simple wardrobe.

Winters were cold in Boston. Her layering of sweaters and sweatpants would frequently put her cousin into horrified shudders because of her lack of fashion sense. "A discussion for another day," she said, smiling at Damen.

"It'll be long and should take place over a lot of wine or bourbon. Whatever's on hand," Damen replied, a wry smile on his lips. He leaned himself back into the couch cushions and raked a hand through his short, tousled hair. "I could talk for days about my father."

Lizzie stepped over to the galley, riffling through the cupboards and drawers. Returning to the table with a bottle of wine and a full bottle of fine bourbon. Damen raised eyebrows, his eyes wide at the sight. "We've got some time and no immediate responsibilities," Lizzie said plunking the bottles onto the table. "But I'm not one drink on an empty stomach. Learned that the hard way. Are you up for some pizza?"

Damen took the bottle from the table, looking carefully at the label. "Sounds good, I'm not much of a drinker, but it's not a bad idea. Not sure what you're planning on, but you spoil me here, Lizzie. Who knows what I'd be eating over on the ship."

She laughed. "Thanks to Marcus, he's the greatest host. He stocked up, knowing my culinary skills would be wanting."

"You've done great for what I've experienced so far. I haven't been poisoned yet."

"Give it time, give it time," Lizzy laughed, preheating the oven. She was relieved that they'd moved back to their easy exchange. Her shoulders relaxed and the earlier tension eased somewhat. She was glad to be near to leaving the island for school again, but she would miss the life of the past couple of weeks. It wasn't the hard work she would miss or the thrill of finding long-lost gold at the bottom of the sea. It was Damen.

She stole a glance at him, still absorbed in reading the label of the bourbon bottle. As if he could hear her thoughts, he raised his eyes to meet hers. Her stomach flipped, and she quickly turned away. "Want ice for that?" she asked, turning away to distract herself.

Drinking alcohol wasn't the best idea to pass the time. It was appealing, however, to break the tension or to grease the way to more bad choices. The thought appealed to him. His attraction to her was eating his insides.

There was an aside to the physical attraction that surprised him. Damen wanted to know more about her, even though he'd known her most of her life. He really didn't know her. She intrigued him. Plus, he really needed to get his mind off of the other parts that had grown into a shapely woman.

Lizzie brought a pair of wine glasses and a glass with ice for the bourbon. "Not having any?" he asked, pouring himself a two-finger share.

"No thanks, not really my taste," she said, her expression that of marked distaste.

He noted the wine was a nice pinot noir. Of course, they *were* on a yacht.

Lizzie took the seat across from him and poured herself a hearty glass of wine and they cordially sipped while waiting for the oven to preheat. "I hope you're hungry," she said. "It's a large pepperoni. There're not any fresh vegetables for a salad, we've used them all up. Just have enough food stock for the next couple of days before we have to leave to go back."

They sat with each other in silence, each with their own thoughts, contemplating the conversation and enjoying their beverages. The boat still rocked in the waves, both quite used to it by now. Even so, he witnessed Lizzie holding on to things as she moved about the cabin, preparing their meal.

"What's next for you, Lizzie?" he asked, curious where her life was going to take her. "I mean, I know that you're headed to medical school. Have you considered what schools to apply to?"

Lizzie gave him a side-ways glance, a sarcastic smile on her lips. "Honestly, it's my father's choice. My first choice will be, of course, Harvard Medical School. I'm likely to get in, of course, because of him."

"I'm sure you've been working hard, don't sell yourself short. Do you have any other choices or are you just limiting yourself to Harvard?" Damen asked, sipping his drink and smiling at her.

"Well," Lizzie replied. "His second choice for me would be the University of Vermont Medical School and the third, the University of Maine."

"No southern schools?" he asked.

Lizzy shrugged and smirked. "Too far away from my father, those were all easy commutes from Boston, should I not get into Harvard. You know... easy oversight."

"I hear you. Here's to involved fathers," Damen replied, reaching over and clinking glasses with her.

"How about you? Is your plan to stay in the service?" Lizzie asked.

"Most definitely," he replied.

"Dangerous work, isn't it?" Lizzie asked. "I mean, if you like that kind of thing, I mean. Aren't you be deployed a lot?"

Damen chuckled, leaning back in his seat, sipping his bourbon. "Yeah, the world is a kind of messed-up place here and there. I like to do something about it. There's more to life than diving for trinkets like my father. He's been searching for treasure his entire life and then doing legal battles with the government to keep any of it. I'd like to make a difference; make it a safer place for everyone."

"That's a noble commitment," she said, gazing at him admiringly.

Damen leaned forward and touched her hand. "So is going to medical school. Lots of years in college, lots of years of learning, nights, weekends. Lots of dedication there."

"I guess we have that in common," she replied. "Wanting to make the world a better place."

They both took a sip of their drinks.

"You mentioned earlier you wanted to go into law instead of medicine? What about that?"

"Yeah," she replied, her face a frown as if she was trying to form the words in her mind. "I'm very interested in discovering new methods in forensics to dig more deeply into investigative processes."

"Your sister's case has a lot to do with that, I assume?" Damen asked. "Couldn't you do that as a doctor?"

Lizzie nodded in agreement, taking another sip from her glass. "My father wants me to be a surgeon like him, so that's off the table if I go into medicine. It's always interested me because it appears, to me anyway, that there were steps taken in that investigation that missed evidence or missed steps to find or take proper procedure to find whatever happened to her," Lizzie said. "I just think it's impossible for somebody to just completely disappear off the face of the earth. Someone has to know something."

"I understand. Trust me, I do. But it seems to happen a lot. Is it just here or is it something with law enforcement altogether?"

She looked at him, her expression deeply serious. "As crazy as it may sound, there are thousands of missing people in the United States alone every year. Some go unreported for days. And with some, there's just no evidence to support whatever happened to them. There's got to be a better way. What are we missing?"

"And you think you can fix that?" Damen asked.

"Somebody should." The buzzer from the oven interrupted their conversation.

Damen was glad Lizzie busied herself in the kitchen and didn't pick up the conversation back to her sister. He was at a loss for what to say without stepping into territory that would derail the conversation. He wanted to get to know her better, not dredge up old memories. It had upset her last night, he'd avoid doing that again.

She served the slices of pizza, and they continued to talk and drink a little. The food was good, and he was starving, so they ate their pizza in silence.

After they finished eating, Damen steered the discussion back to lighter topics, and they fell into an easy conversation. The hours moved on and they played a few more games of cards, resuming their friendly competition.

After a while, and several more dollars in the hole, Lizzie appeared to be feeling her wine. Damen noted she had re-filled her glass several times and more than half of the bottle of wine was gone. She had to be feeling the effects of the alcohol. Her laugh had grown easier and her eyes brighter as the evening wore on. He was feeling very relaxed and at ease himself after two glasses of bourbon.

Lizzie shuffled the deck of cards in her hands and took a deep breath, appearing to gain confidence from the fresh air. She placed the cards on the table and leaned back on the couch, looking directly at him. "I suppose we should probably clear the air about last night," she said, her tone serious.

His stomach fluttered in a warning; he placed his palms flat on the smooth surface. The voice in his head cautioning him. "There's no need to talk about it. You were upset with the anniversary of your sister and all."

Her gaze leveled him. "No, I mean, about kissing you."

"And I kissed you," he replied, his voice husky. His lower body recalling all too easily how she had felt in his arms.

She blushed, the color rising to her cheeks. He could feel the heat rising in her, just across the small table. His mind thought about reaching over the table and laying her on top of it and ... *Where was this coming from?*

"I really don't want you to think that I'm a bad person," she said. "I wouldn't hurt Daniel for the world."

It was as if cold ice splashed on him at the mention of his brother's name. "You *are* his girl..."

They looked into each other's eyes, both uneasy about the conversation. He wanted to both pull her into his arms and push her away; the conflict growing in him.

"It's complicated," she said, her voice trailing into a sigh.

Damen raised an eyebrow.

"I just wanted to clear the air on the subject. I'm not that kind of person, not that kind of girl."

Lizzie rose to her feet, tottering in the boat's movement, and the effect of the wine. Damen jumped up to steady her and found her in his arms.

It was as if his body had its own idea. Finding her crushed against him, her soft curves conforming to his lean muscles. Fire burned in his gut. He wanted her. How they could go from easy camaraderie to immediate fire puzzled him. *She* confused him, but he wanted to explore more of this.

He expected her to push him away, yet her hands slid up his arms to grasp his shoulders. She tipped her head back to look up into his face, her eyes dark and sparkling in the dim light, her lips full and promising.

He couldn't resist her and reached down to plunder her mouth with his own. Surprised, she stilled, and then pressed herself closer, opening her mouth to his, giving herself to the kiss. His mouth took her in, tasting the wine on her lips. His hands roamed her body, cupping her buttocks and pulling her ever closer to his hardening body. He wanted her more than anything. His hands slid up her back, pulling the clothing from her skin. Her sigh pulled him back.

He pushed her away from him, holding her at arm's length from his burning skin. "If you weren't my brother's girl, Lizzie, I would take you below right now."

Her eyes widened, her hands straightening her clothing. "Would you want that?" he asked.

"Yes," she whispered, her voice husky. "But no." She stepped back from him.

There it was. She wanted him, but wouldn't cheat on his brother.

There was only one solution. He released her. "Go to bed Lizzie. And lock your door."

CHAPTER II

The weather had finally broken, and the seas were calm enough to dive by the next morning. Lizzie woke to the roaring of the yacht's engines as Damen re-positioned the boat back in its place next to the yacht. By the time she came out on deck, he'd boarded the *Merchant* and was working with the crew. She'd wait until he signaled he was ready to dive to gear up. Her equipment was ready for her on the deck. Damen had apparently been up prepping early that morning, as her tanks were ready and full, and dive gear laid out.

Her thoughts stayed on their interaction of the previous night. Although she'd had more than enough wine, the kiss was clear in her mind. Sipping her coffee, her thoughts moved to what could have happened between them, if she hadn't followed his direction and gone to her berth. The rough feeling of his beard on her skin as he kissed her came into her mind, making her wonder how that would have felt on other parts of her body.

"You gearing up?" A voice boomed from across the short distance to the *Merchant*, yanking her from her fantasies.

Lizzie looked over to the rusted boat where Damen stood glaring at her in the early morning sunlight. She shook off her thoughts and quickly donned her gear to join him in the water. Trying to get her mind back into the dive and the teamwork they'd developed under the surface. Before she could get into the water, he'd swam over to the yacht.

Apparently, the frogman life suited him well, being able to gear up so quickly. He'd been born into it, literally. Damen easily climbed up on the beach deck of the catamaran and helped Lizzie with her tanks, re-checking gauges and equipment. Safety was paramount to him, and it was apparent his military training had taken that to a higher level than what his father had instilled over the years. It was a paradox that Isaac's diving safety rules didn't match up with that of how the man treated the general equipment of his businesses with the rusted boats and malfunctioning equipment. It was more likely the cause of which was tied to the lack of funding rather than the lack of attention.

Lizzie stilled her thoughts. It wouldn't do to have them distract her from the business at hand. They moved easily now through their dive; she followed him on the descent through the warm water to the wreck below.

The sand beneath the surface looked vastly different from when they'd first discovered her. Now it was as though they had bared the old ship's bones, with her ribcage easily seen with the remnants of timbers cleared on sand on the bottom. Potholes and craters covered the surface where the crew had cleared artifacts and treasure from her hold. They had hauled uncounted amounts of silver and gold to the surface over the past weeks, and there was still more to be found. Lizzie wouldn't be there to see it.

The recent storm had left the wreck site undisturbed, even though the waves above had been rough. Lizzie thought of the hurricane forming thousands of miles away and wondered if it would affect the salvage activities. It was again something not of her concern, her work would be done here.

In a way, she wished they could go on like this forever, but things had changed between them. Life needed to move forward.

Ahead of her in the murky water, Damen fanned his hands over an untouched area of smooth sand covering rocks or other objects. The area was just outside of the already excavated sand, so likely to wield more finds or to show there was nothing to be found in that location. The process they followed was pretty scientific. Lizzie had marveled at the overall methods of excavation and systematic cataloging of the finds.

The history of the wreck was fascinating to consider. The most interesting was that the wreck had been here for hundreds of years, and no one had found her until the day she and Damen did. Truly, it was like finding a needle in a haystack. It was great when it happened, but how long had Isaac been searching for her, how many people had been injured or lost for the sake of finding treasure, of *maybe* finding treasure? She was glad that Damen and Daniel both were not eager to follow in their father's footsteps because of that uncertainty, and banking a business, a family and a life on it as Isaac had done and continued to do. The reality of the life was something else entirely, although it may sound adventurous to some.

As she swam over the wreck, fanning the sand here and there with her hands, her mind drifted to stories her mother had told her of her family long ago. Her Spanish ancestors had been lost in a storm on their way back to their motherland, since then her family had stayed in Cuba. There was a vague story of a great grandmother who had left her young family behind in Cuba to meet her husband's aristocratic family in the old world. Her portrait hung in their home.

Although Lizzie admittedly did not pay great attention to the overall story or the portrait that blended in with the life, she struggled now to remember the details.

It would be amazing to possess the necklace, particularly if it had a connection to her ancestors, lost at sea. There was another reason she wanted to have it; its meaning deeper than she liked to admit. And that was it would cause her mother to take notice and consider what Lizzie had been doing. Preserving the history of her heritage. Getting her mother's attention was something that she had strived to accomplish ever since her sister went missing. But nothing had stirred the older woman, nothing since before her older daughter had disappeared.

The lack of her mother's love and attention was a hole in Lizzie's heart. It wasn't exactly that her mother didn't love her; but more the absence of display and caring that would emanate from her friends' mothers and not her own. There was a vacant spot that was waiting to be filled inside of her. Lizzy knew, after several years of therapy urged by her father, that it was why she still, to this day, pursued the mystery of her sister. It was as though if she could find the answers, her mother would love her, the way she had loved Cami. It was also the reason that her father firmly discouraged her from pursuing career options in law enforcement or forensics, feeling it stemmed from the attempt to fill in the emotional vacancy.

Lizzie's father stepped in to fill the gap left by her mother's indifference. She wondered if he experienced the same gap from his wife, with the longer lengths of time he spent away from home working and had insisted Lizzie spend as well. She was glad to have to only spend a few days of what she had left of her summer vacation back in her parent's house. The undercurrent of their failing relationship wore at her like an unhealing wound. She'd like them to just end it, if that was what they were ultimately going to do.

Knowing her thoughts distracted her, Lizzie forced herself to pay attention to Damen's position in the water.. His bubbles were easy to follow, and she caught up to him with ease. He handed her some conglomerate which resembled some kind of tool. Lizzie placed it in her dive bag to bring up for the archeologist to work through.

Shortly, Damen handed her another object, stilling himself in the water at her side while she examined the find. It was a beautiful and rare Junonia shell, empty of its occupant. The lovely shell with its leopard spotted appearance was a rarity to find on a beach, even uncommon at these depths. Lizzie had never seen once so large, it had to be four or five inches long. The tourist shell seekers sought after them. Damen watched her face as she examined the shell, knowing her delight was obvious to him.

Damen gestured to her he was giving it to her as a gift. Lizzie slipped the shell into her suit, careful to avoid crushing it, touched by the uncharacteristic display from him. Typically, he was all business when they were on a dive. Perhaps he, too, was thinking of their last evening and the end of their time together.

He swam off, and she followed his stream of bubbles, resuming their search for further artifacts. Lizzie followed, her mind continuing to drift with the upcoming days back in town, the tasks ahead, and what the sheriff's deputy had to report, if she would finally have some answers to Cami's disappearance.

CHAPTER 12

Daniel stood on the deck of the *Merchant,* his tousled hair blowing freely in the wind. Lizzie admired his good looks and looked for similarities with Damen. They were half-brothers and looked nothing alike. However, with study, there were some subtleties that would have gone unnoticed if she hadn't spent the last few weeks working and living so closely with Damen.

"You look good Lizzie. This sea air must agree with you," Daniel said, leaning back on his crutches and looking down at her.

"That and an awful lot of hard work." she replied, happy to see him.

"I hope Damen wasn't the drill master he's known to be. He can be relentless," Daniel said, glancing toward the boathouse where Damen and his father were having a heated discussion.

"He was really okay to work with. It definitely wasn't what I was expecting, but the finds were really fascinating. I can see why people get caught up in the treasure hunt."

Daniel smiled widely, his surfer boy grin. "Catch the bug now? Going to be a treasure hunter now? Or maybe you've taken a liking to my frogman brother."

Lizzie felt her color rise at his teasing and knew if Daniel was paying any attention, he'd catch it. "I wonder what's up,"

Lizzie said, gesturing to the now very heated argument the two men were having.

"Yeah..... nothing new, with those two could be anything really..... Lizzie. Are you blushing?"

Daniel leaned his face down closer to hers as so not to be overheard. "There's nothing I'd like better to have you stay in my family, but Lizzie, he's a tough nut. He can be a bear to be around on his good days. Be sure if you step in that direction, he's not the type to play around and.... neither are you."

"Nothing to worry about there. We're leaving. He's leaving. There's not a chance. He's also too honorable to cheat on his brother."

Daniel stood up straight, his lips a thin line. "I've stood in your way again."

Lizzie shook her head, taking his hand, brushing his knuckles to her lips. "No, you haven't. It's for the best, anyway. It wouldn't have worked out, long distance relationship and all."

Daniel ran his free hand tenderly over her cheek and down her shoulder to pull her into an embrace. "Ahh Lizzie, you are the best. I love you so. Someday, we'll be ready. Someday soon."

She knew that when Daniel and Marcus were ready to reveal themselves to their families, they would. It was such a traumatic situation; to not share your true self with family. Lizzie knew both men grappled with challenging emotions, withholding coming out altogether. All she could do was support them and be there for them when they needed her, her two best friends since childhood. She couldn't imagine life without them.

Daniel kissed her forehead and released her. Damen cleared his throat loudly behind them. His face was unreadable, covered mostly by sunglasses. A muscle worked in his jaw as he watched them. Anger flowed from him. Lizzie knew it wasn't focused on them, but on the man who was pulling away from the ship in his boat, their father.

"What's up, bro? Pops, get under your skin?" Daniel joked.

Damen shook his head, his gaze following Isaac's wake. "Sorry about that, man. He must have woken up like that this morning. I heard it all the way out here. I can assure that you are not the only son he's disappointed in." Daniel reached out to pat his older brother on his shoulder.

"A few more days," Damen said softly, "just a few more days...."

"I got this one for you, bro. Go ahead in, get yourself together. I can handle it from here, only for a few more days for all of us, anyway."

"Do you know if he was lying about the *Viking?* Will it really be ready in a few days, and with the crew?"

"Yeah, I really don't know what the old man's up to. But the thing is, I don't need to. I got to be back at school. The year's all paid up. And you've got to get back to saving the world. Isaac will do what Isaac's always done."

Damen's gaze scrutinized Daniel, leaning on his crutches, the walking boot cast. "Are you sure you're up for this? The crew is short already, and with Lizzie and I leaving even more so. Will you be able to get around all right?"

The frown between Damen's eyes deepened as he considered his little brother. Lizzie shared the concern. Walking around a boat rocking in the waves was hard enough without an injured leg. It would be difficult for Daniel to get around. He wouldn't be diving, as he was supposed to keep the leg dry. Bacteria from the water getting in his wound would not be a healthy thing. However, his doctor felt it would be fine medically if he followed instructions.

"No worries. I'll be overseeing things. I'll stay high and dry. For a couple of days, I can do anything."

Damen shoved his hands in his pockets, his eyes downcast, considering. "There's a lot to show you on this hunk of junk. The crew that's staying behind knows all the in's and out's and how to make things run. But you should know them as well. You know, to *oversee* everything."

Lizzie visibly relaxed at Damen's half smile. Daniel had that impact, his ability to make light of serious situations. It was nice to see Damen was not immune to his little brother's warming personality.

The two men walked away to the pilothouse, one limping but joking the entire way. Lizzie followed, determined to make the accommodations for Daniel as comfortable as possible and adapt the surroundings as much as possible to account for his physical limitations. There was no need for him to suffer, there were ways to make it easier.

Several hours later, Lizzie and Damen were headed in with the yacht. Damen was piloting, and they were taking their time, not pushing the boat. They would arrive at port on Stock Island before sunset, where Marcus kept the yacht. The slower pace allowed Damen the space to think, and to clear his mind from the disruption of his father earlier in the day.

It had been a classic Isaac move to ignore Damen's advice to bring the *Merchant* back into port for repairs and replace the ship with the *Viking* and crew. He had a lame excuse that the ship wasn't ready or something. Damen knew deep down that his father was trying to save a few dollars by bringing the *Viking* out at the last minute. It was that, or he'd pissed someone off already. The latter was less likely, as Damen knew, people would put up with Isaac now, with the reality of the treasure being a true factor. Divers and crew knew he would pay them, and well, now they had finally located the *Atocha*. The dream and promise had transitioned into reality and fact, and a small percentage of the salvage.

Damen glanced at Lizzie. She preferred to be nearby on deck when the boat was in motion; he'd noticed. She gazed out to sea, and he wondered if she was thinking of Daniel. A pang of jealousy struck him. He'd paid attention to their exchange on deck, having not done so for years, seeing them together in the background of his life for so long. They were sweet with each other, he'd observed. But there had been no passionate greeting and no long kiss goodbye. His brother had warmly kissed her cheek as they embraced. There was no deep emotion on display, just a sweet tenderness between them. Had they been together so long they were already like a long-married couple?

Lizzie had been attentive to ensure that they adapted the overall accommodations as best they could to ensure Daniel's comfort. He'd be bunking in the cramped pilot house in order to avoid the narrow stairs to the berths below. As most spent their nights on deck anyway, it wasn't a big change. She'd overseen the re-arranging of some miscellaneous deck equipment and located a rolling chair from below. He was all set up to accommodate his injury.

Damen still didn't like the whole idea, not that it really was his responsibility any longer. Daniel was well liked by the crew, and easygoing enough that they would get some work done, regardless. There would be people to help Daniel if he were to get into trouble, and he would accept their help. He'd shown Daniel the challenges with the *Merchant*, and the patchwork of temporary repairs they'd done. Damen doubted that Daniel really paid attention and would rely on the crew to continue to do the work they had been doing all along to hold things together.

They predicted the weather to be calm for the next few days, even though all eyes were still tracking the developing storm out to sea. It hadn't formed into a hurricane yet, but it was a growing tropical storm. This gave Daniel yet another reprieve, and he wouldn't be struggling to stay upright in rough seas, nor have to worry about the bilge pumps not keeping up.

All would be well with Daniel; however, he couldn't shake the feeling of unease. His eyes rested again on Lizzie. Perhaps she was the reason for his feelings of disquiet. Their attraction still burned in him, and she was all he could think about. In a few brief hours, they wouldn't have to see each other again and he'd be away from the temptation of her. He should feel relief, but he didn't.

Deployment was scheduled to begin a few days after his leave ended. In a short time, he'd be taking off to an unknown location. He looked forward to being reunited with his team, his brothers. It was a hard job, a hard life, but it was all his. There wasn't room in it for someone else. It wouldn't be fair to her, or to himself. If the circumstances of his life were different, he would contemplate a relationship with her or someone like her at some point. Some of his teammates had families and lives beyond their work. It was possible.

He watched her closely, mesmerized by the way the wind blew her hair around her face. She was stunningly beautiful, and he wondered if she knew just how beautiful she was. Most women he knew who were aware of their assets flaunted them, using their wardrobe and make-up to enhance their features. Lizzie did none of those things. Another reason for the attraction was that he'd seen her genuine self over the past couple of weeks, and it drew him to her. The smattering of freckles across her nose, and the way her eyes sparkled when she laughed, all ran through his mind.

They'd be back to shore soon. He was likely to not lay eyes on her for years, if ever again. A sudden hole felt ripped in his gut. He knew all too well how short life was, how in one moment you could be present and then gone in the next. The service had taught him that all too well. Even though he had a dangerous job, willingly stepping into a firefight when needed, he appreciated the preciousness of life.

Damen reduced the speed of the yacht and shut off the engines. The sudden quiet brought Lizzie out of her thoughts. She turned to him. "Is everything all right?" she asked, shading her eyes from the sun.

Damen stood to face her, his heart racing. "No. It's not all right."

Her expression changed from questioning to apprehension as Damen approached her, taking her hand is his as he slid next to her on the bench. "It's likely we won't see each other for a very long time, if at all. And I don't want to leave without one last taste of you."

He reached out and took her face in his hands, his eyes on her full lips. "I know there can't be anything between us, but grant me this one ... last... kiss."

She hesitated a micro-second as she absorbed his meaning. Then she reached up and pulled his lips to hers. His stomach flipped as her lips touched his own, filling him with a smoldering heat. He'd pushed the feelings away, trying to avoid them, trying to save himself from betraying his brother, but they rose in him again. He'd never wanted another woman as he wanted her.

They kissed passionately, her lips parting for his tongue as he pulled her deeper against his chest. He couldn't stop himself, as his lips found her earlobe, causing her to shiver in his arms, her soft moan nearly causing him to burst. He found her neck as she slipped into his lap, straddling him, his tightening pants pushing against her shorts, her long legs on each side of his. His hands ran up her buttocks, up her smooth back, and under the gauzy shirt she wore, both hands cupping her breasts.

Lizzie arched her back, thrusting her breasts forward, the fabric parting for his mouth to find her nipple. She sighed once more, and he was undone. Throwing all caution to the wind, he laid her on her back on the bench, covering her with his burning body. She kissed him, her hands roaming on his body, pushing away the fabric of his shirt to run her hands over his bare chest.

His lips continued their exploration of her skin, devouring her breasts, while his hands roamed to her shorts. Slipping his hand inside her clothing, he found her hot and wet. She whispered his name.

The loud blare of a horn startled him, causing him to freeze in place.

Remembering where he was, and that they were in full view of passersby, he rose to his feet, straightening his clothes. To his surprise, there was a Coast Guard Defender boat pulled alongside. When he shut off the engines, there was no one in sight. He was certain that there wasn't another boat nearby, but the model of their boat could traverse the water swiftly.

"Hello!" Damen called.

"Everything all right? Having engine trouble?" called the skipper.

"No sorry, we're good here, heading into port," Damen responded. He recognized one man on the boat.

"Having a lot of trouble lately with refugees, had a report of a boat in the area. See anything on your way?"

"Not a thing. I'll let you know if we see anything on the way back," Damen answered.

The men reeved their engines and pulled away quickly from the yacht. He admired their tenacity and speed around the area. The Cuban refugees had recently become more of an issue because of the decline in the economy in their country. It was always something, drug trafficking, refugees, pirates... life on the high seas.

He turned to look back at Lizzie. She was flushed, but had readjusted her clothing, crossing her legs and arms as she sat on the bench.

Damen ran his hand through his hair. He had to stay away from her, or he'd have her naked and under him in the next few minutes. He'd intended to kiss her, not make love to her. Clearly, that was where they were headed just moments ago.

He started the engines, glancing back at her as he pulled the boat back onto their course. "I'm sorry. I.."

She nodded, observing him. "That was some goodbye kiss," she said, rising to her feet.

He looked over at her and saw she was smiling. Her mouth quirked in humor. "I'll see you when we get back."

She carefully made her way down the steps to the main deck, disappearing from view. It disappointed Damen with her leaving, however; he knew it was for the best. Soon they would be away from each other for good, and this temptation would no longer be a concern.

CHAPTER 13

"Everything all right?" Marcus asked, speeding through the narrow streets of the old town. He was a maniac behind the wheel, as usual, sending tourists scrambling out of his way.

Marcus had picked her up dockside. Lizzie imagined he was now at a loss for things to do with Daniel offshore for a few more days. "Sure, why do you ask?"

Marcus grinned. "Seems like you and the beast have made friends. At least that's what I would call it, anyway. He looked like he wanted to eat you."

Lizzie replied with a thin-lipped smile, attempting to be evasive, as Marcus would turn any hint of interest into a big deal. Not something she wanted, not even sure herself what it was between them. Damen's attempt at a goodbye kiss, and her response to him, both thrilled and scared her. Although there had been boyfriends in her life, away at school, none had kissed her in that way or had drawn her passion to the surface so quickly. He drew her to him. His touch caused fire to rage in her belly and an apparent willingness to throw caution to the wind. What would have happened if the Coast Guard vessel hadn't hailed them? A tingle rose her spine, and her stomach flipped.

She sighed. Now she would never know. Both were headed in a different direction in their lives. Damen was still under the impression that she and Daniel were together and would likely never try to touch her again. If she ever saw him again.

Marcus had offered him a ride, which he turned down. Apparently, he was going to catch up with the crew of the *Viking*. For someone who wanted to no longer engage with his father's business, he didn't seem like the uninterested party. Damen's earlier argument with his father over his choice to delay the needed repairs for the *Merchant*, really seemed to eat at him.

"Not dishing, little cousin?" Marcus asked teasingly. "No worries, I think the young deputy has been looking for you, so you won't be short a date this weekend."

Lizzie playfully smacked him on the knee. "Have you seen him?"

"I saw him when I was out walking the other day. He was looking to see when you were coming back. Asked that I have you call him when you do." Marcus pulled his car up to the front of her parent's home and leaned over to look at her, his tone serious. "I worry about you when it comes to Cami's disappearance. So much time has passed, there's not likely to be anything new... it won't change what the likely outcome has been..."

She looked into his face, her long-time best friend and cousin. They were tied together, long before Cami's disappearance, part of the same family and familiar dynamic. He understood her, and her relationship with her parents like no one else could. His own absentee family had him turning to her. They were bound, as brother and sister, and she loved him. His kind and caring ways had gotten her through the early years and continued to now with this recent evidence that had arisen. "I'll be okay. I'll call you if there's anything of significance."

"Ashley was asking about you, too. Call her before we go back. You know how she gets when she feels left out," Marcus said, dropping his seriousness. "If she hears anything has been found, she'll want to do a seance or a Ouija board session."

They both laughed together for a moment. "She's really gotten into that now...." Lizzie said.

"Big business with the tourists. They have a couple of drinks and want to hear their future or try to contact the dead," Marcus replied, shaking his head. "She's doing really well, though. Call her seriously, Lizzie. You've been friends for so long, and you need more than me and Daniel."

"Nice try. You just want her to stop bothering you," Lizzie said, smiling at her cousin. Marcus and Ashley never really melded well, creating the need to keep their friendships separate from her perspective. Ashley had a thing for Marcus ever since they were little, and had dreams of becoming a couple with him, as Daniel and Lizzie supposedly were. Marcus worried she would discover his true nature, outing him before he was ready to come out himself. Keeping his distance was in his best interest.

Lizzie kissed her cousin on his cheek. "Don't worry, I will."

"Don't forget to pack. I'm shipping some things up the day before we go. Let me know if there's anything you want to send," he said as she gathered her things from the car.

"Will do. See you tomorrow. Sure, you don't want to come in?" she asked, looking for a buffer with her parents. Both cars were in the driveway, both were home.

He shook his head, smiling back at her. "No, thanks!"

Lizzie slung her bag over her shoulder, waving to Marcus as he pulled away.

The lights were on in the house, illuminating the large windows of the Spanish Colonial-style house. She sighed, resigning herself to the conversation she knew awaited her inside.

"I don't like you hanging around with that man, Lizzie. Daniel is one thing, but staying out for weeks working for *that man,*" her mother said, sipping on her martini.

It was late for her mother to be drinking, typically she kept to her schedule of cocktails at six, with or without company. Her father leaned in the doorway, neither in nor out of the room. *Planning for his quick escape*, she thought.

Lizzie checked her phone, which had been buzzing non-stop with texts since she arrived back on land. Both Paul Nichols, the deputy and her friend Ashley were eager to see her tonight.

"You realize that man is grave robbing, and likely from your own ancestors? Joining him in that endeavor is not something I approve of in the least." Soledad's tone left nothing to the imagination. She disapproved of the Wisler's altogether.

Lizzie's hand moved to the necklace she wore, covered by her t-shirt. She'd forgotten and worn the necklace back after trying it on earlier in the morning. It still fascinated her how it was unflawed after being at the bottom of the sea for multiple centuries.

"Isaac said you would say that," Lizzie started, noting her father's attention shifting to her words. "He wanted to be sure I showed you a piece I found while diving. It has to go back for cataloging and appraisal, along with the rest of the treasure. Eventually, it'll be mine."

She unclasped the necklace, holding it out for her mother's inspection. Soledad set her martini aside, intrigued by the jewelry. The emerald cross glinted in the lamplight as her mother fingered the object. Her father stepped closer for inspection. "It looks brand new," her mother whispered.

Rising quickly from her seat, Soledad took the necklace from Lizzie's hands, and paced to the formal dining room, seldom used by their family. She stood gazing up at a portrait of a young woman Lizzie knew to be an ancestor from Cuba. "Look here, such a resemblance," Soledad muttered to Lizzie and her father, who had followed her into the room.

The painting was old, the paint's color fading from age, but around the neck of its somber eyed subject hung an emerald cross very like the one hanging now in her mother's hand. A chill ran up Lizzie's spine.

Soledad shoved the necklace back at Lizzie. "He *should* give it to you. It's yours. It was her's, your great grandmother from centuries ago. She left her young children behind to sail to Spain to meet her husband's family and drowned in the hurricane. It's her grave you've been digging in."

Soledad turned dramatically on her heel, leaving Lizzie and her father in stunned silence, shattered moments later by the slamming of her mother's bedroom door.

CHAPTER 14

Lizzie swirled her finger in the condensation on her wineglass. Paul had texted and said he was running behind. He'd join her shortly. She was glad for a moment of peace, the out of the way café was quiet tonight, and gave her a chance to catch her breath after the drama with her mother.

She'd grown to expect such dramatic outbursts from her mother, but somehow this one got under her skin. Swimming through the wreckage, she had the same thoughts. Concerns about the passengers who perished on the ship, holding on for their lives, knowing they were doomed as the waves lashed their ship. Her fingers found the necklace, and she wondered about the owner. Lizzie had discovered the chain in a jewelry box, as though placed there purposefully waiting for centuries for someone to locate it. Had her ancestor done that when she knew she was doomed? A chill ran up her spine, despite the warm evening.

A kiss on her cheek startled her out of her thoughts, and nearly spilling her wine. "Oh, sorry, didn't mean to scare you," Paul said, slipping into the seat opposite hers. "You look like you're a million miles away."

"Hundreds of years," Lizzie joked, trying to regain her composure.

Paul grasped her hand earnestly, leaning eagerly forward. "You look good, Lizzie. Looks like you've been taking in some sun. Beautiful as always."

She smiled at him, patiently accepting the physical contact. Even though she'd made it clear frequently that a relationship with him wasn't possible, he still continued to pursue her, ever hopeful. Lizzie tolerated it, pushing him back whenever he crossed lines. He was her only source of information currently on Cami's case and she didn't want to further jeopardize access to information.

"Thank you. I was out helping the salvage operation." She leaned back in her chair, to add space between them.

"I heard you did that. Daniel is out there now, right?"

She wasn't surprised that he had this information, and noted he hadn't released her fingers. "We leave the day after tomorrow."

At her tone, Paul withdrew his hand and hailed a server to place his drink order. "So soon," he replied, reaching into his pocket to retrieve his phone, scrolling through messages before locating what he came to discuss with her.

Lizzie braced herself, knowing there was likely to not be much of anything new in her sister's case. There was always hope for an answer to what happened that day.

Paul took her hand again, looking seriously into her face. "There was DNA on the bathing suit material, Lizzie. It was a match for your sister. And there was more. Another person's DNA was found as well...." He hesitated, giving her a chance to absorb what he was saying.

Immediately, Lizzie's head spun. It was hers; it was Cami's! It was something that they hadn't had a break in years. "Do they have a match for the other DNA?"

"As far as I know, and the Sherriff is keeping this close, there isn't a match."

"What does that mean?" she asked, her voice becoming anxious. It sounded as though they would come this far, and no further.

"It just means that there is not a match for anyone in the system." He explained gently, retaking her hand and squeezing her fingers a little too hard.

"And they still haven't found anything else at the site, where they found the suit?" Lizzie asked, carefully choosing her words. She wanted to know, but also didn't.

Paul shook his head and held his tongue while the server placed a beer with lime in front of him, waiting until she left the table. "There was a review of the site, but because of the time that's passed, there was nothing there. If there had been, it could have easily been washed away over the years. Finding this one piece of evidence was sheer luck, including it having any DNA on it at all."

Lizzie nodded. It was one thing she knew and had heard repeatedly. The beach where her sister disappeared was full of people on most days, with it being outside, in a tropical area, with rain, wind and time covering up any evidence. It had been like she disappeared off the face of the earth that day until now.

"Of course, having her suit there that she was wearing for work could mean many things. Did she change and leave with someone in a car or a boat? Who and why?"

The implication wasn't lost on Lizzie. There had been conjectures early on about the possibility of human traffickers, or murderous rapists. Still, there had been no clue, no shred of evidence, that this had been the case. There had been no sign that Cami was alive somewhere, living with another family, a boyfriend, or on her own.

"Something, but just more questions," Lizzie sighed, thinking it wasn't enough information to bring to her parents.

Paul leaned back in his seat, taking a deep pull from his beer. He studied her face, as though considering his words. "There's something else... it may just be a coincidence. I'm almost not even sure I should bring it up."

Lizzie's stomach flipped at the thought of something further he may have found. "There was a car reported stolen a few days prior to your sister's disappearance. It may be nothing, and I followed up on it on a hunch the other night when it was slow. You know the bridges all have cameras...?"

"Yes, yes. There's something...?" Lizzie urged him on. It was his style to string out any information he'd tell her. It was likely a way to have more time with her.

"The timing was right, and the photo is... well, it's inconclusive, really. I almost didn't want to bring it up, raise your hopes and all that..." Paul said, scrolling through his phone before locating the footage he was referring to.

He scooted his chair to be closer to hers, their thighs brushing as he leaned into her to view the screen on his phone. "It's hard to make out, but here's that car, passing through the bridge. The driver."

Lizzie's breath caught in her throat. The photo was grainy, taken at night, but it was clearly the shape of a head with hair brushing the shoulders in the same way that Cami wore her hair. The driver's face shrouded in darkness; they could see no distinguishing facial features. It was familiar, however, with the hairstyle. It could be her... which would mean she had left. She'd left them all wondering what happened to her.

"Before you jump to conclusions, Lizzie, I will tell you I couldn't use this photo for any kind of identification. It's just not clear enough to ID the driver, but it was definitely the stolen car."

"Was the car ever located?" she asked, hopeful for more information.

"That's the other thing with this, and yet another reason I hesitated to bring it to you. That's the thing. The car's never been recovered, and to add to it. It's never been flagged leaving the Keys, either."

"It never left the Keys, and it was never located? Where did it go?" Lizzie asked, confused. There was only one way in or out of the Keys by car, on the roads and bridges.

"I think this is why it was never pursued by the formal investigation. It's yet another mystery if this is even all connected. There may be a chop shop somewhere in the Keys that law enforcement doesn't know about, but I sincerely doubt it," Paul said, taking another swig from his beer.

"Isn't it odd that a stolen car never shows up like that? Where could it have gone?"

Paul smirked, putting his phone away. "There are as many ways as possible to trick law enforcement and conceal detection. It's possible it just wasn't picked up on any of the cameras, plates changed, maybe a quick paint job and all of that."

Lizzie sat back in her seat, deflated. Hoping that this would be something to finally lead them somewhere in Cami's case. There was new information, but nothing that led anywhere new. She'd learned to not expect much, but was still disappointing.

Paul swigged his beer, nearly downing half the bottle. Sweat beaded on his brow. "Will you stay in touch with me

Lizzie again, while you're away? You never know if there's something I find. I'd like to reach out to you. Maybe I could visit Boston. I've been wanting to take a vacation at some point. Maybe we could meet up?"

Irritation rose in her. She was unhappy with herself for expecting something from this charade with Paul. Little bits and pieces of information were all she got, but it was better than the enormous bunch of nothing she received from the sheriff for as many years. She toyed with the thought of dropping it altogether, wait until she was settled into a job and could use her own money for a private investigator to find any information. If she wanted anything in the interim, her only current chose was to maintain the connection to Paul. She sighed; he wasn't really all that bad, just too earnest in his interest in her. She needed to deter him from visiting her in Boston. That would be too much to put up with. It was enough she spent time with him while she was home.

"Yes, yes, of course we'll stay in touch. I'm not so sure I'll have time for a visit, with this being my last year, and applying to medical school...

"I understand." He leaned back in his seat, relieved when she nodded her agreement. "Oh, there is one last thing you should know. That car was owned by your aunt."

The incense burned Lizzie's nose as she waited in the dim light of Ashley's studio for her to finish up with a last-minute reading. The outer shop was filled with trinkets and crystals, books on witchcraft and psychics. It appeared that Madame

Roberta, as she dubbed herself, was doing well in her business.

Ashley had always had been drawn to the occult side of life. Her mother and grandmother had led her in that direction with their own practices set up in the same storefront. Ashley lived upstairs in the quaint house, just off the main Duval Street. The real estate alone had to be worth a fortune, but it was all Ashley's now with her mother retired up to Fort Lauderdale and her grandmother gone for over a decade.

Another child following in her parent's footsteps, but Ashley has done so willingly. It had been her life calling to step into her mother's shoes and run the psychic boutique the same way it had been since her grandmother ran it. Of course, now people were more attuned to the occult with the television shows and ghost hunting spectaculars. She imagined it had changed the tenor of the business. A shiver ran up Lizzie's spine, remembering that Ashley had always loved to reach out to the dead. As a teen, her Ouija board was always close by, but Lizzie couldn't recall a time where any contact had been genuine, with them all explainable.

Lizzie envied Ashley in her acceptance of her parent's plans for her future. It would be easy to just relax and let them lead the way, which is really what Lizzie was doing, letting her father lead her career path. At least she was letting him run it until she could pursue what she truly wanted.

Ashley's path had not been one without its own set of potholes, she reminded herself, wandering the room admiring the mystical display. Early mistakes had led to a very young teen pregnancy. Ashley had ended putting the baby up for adoption, with Lizzie's father's discrete help. A young couple in Maine had adopted her baby girl. It had been gruesomely hard for Ashley, and a short time after Cami's disappearance.

The family stayed in touch with the birth mother on a limited basis with the open adoption. It had been very difficult for the teen, and Lizzie wondered if she still stayed in touch, following her child's growth. She had admired her friend's strength through the entire process, not sure she could have done the same had she been in her shoes.

A customer emerged from the back room, leaving quickly out the front door. Ashley followed with her flowing skirts and jangling bracelets. "So sorry to keep you waiting," she said to Lizzie, flipping the lock on the shop door and turning on the 'closed' sign.

"No worries, knowing the future trumps meeting an old friend," Lizzie said, hugging her friend.

"You look great! Being out on the boats really agrees with you!" Ashley said. "How was Daniel's brother to work with? I hear the guys call him 'the beast.'"

Lizzie raised an eyebrow at her.

"I stopped by with some brownies," Ashley said, shrugging her shoulder. "I heard Daniel had been hurt and thought you could use some sugar. I was surprised to find Marcus there instead of you, of course. But they filled me in."

Of course, you did, Lizzie thought. If she didn't tell her, she'd find out herself, not one to miss out on an opportunity to see Marcus.

"He was actually fine," Lizzie started.

"Mmmm, he sure is fine..." Ashley said, lifting her eyebrow back at her.

Ashley led her into the back room, through the door to her private residence. All the while, she stripping off her many bracelets, and peeling off the flowing skirts until it left her in a tank top and shorts. No longer Madam Roberta, but her old friend Ashley Roberts.

She filled two wineglasses with a generous pour and guided Lizzie to her overstuffed couch filled with colorful pillows. "I know you don't have much time before you go back to school, but I had to see you before you left. I had a dream."

Lizzie stiffened. She'd heard this from her friend hundreds of times, always indulging her and listening to their contents. They were *just* dreams, after all.

"No, really, I know what you're thinking. But this was so real..." Ashley sat back in the cushions and sipped her wine before continuing. "It was one of those dreams that you feel everything, every whisper of the breeze across your skin, every drop of water."

Lizzie took a taste of her drink. "You've had those before, you know..." she said, smiling at her friend.

Ashley plunked her glass down on the table, staring at her friend. "No, no, this was something else. It... it terrified me."

Lizzie could see she was serious; this had upset her. "What was it about?"

Ashley sat back in her seat, taking up her glass again. "I had this dream before I knew you were out on the dive boat. That's why I stopped by. But because you were out there, it made me worry...."

Intrigued, Lizzie sat forward on the couch, reaching out to touch her friend's knee. The movement causing the necklace she wore to slip from under the neckline of her shirt, and dangle between the two women. Instantly, Ashley jolted as though she had been shocked. "Where'd you get that?" she asked, her eyes wide. She reached up to finger the emerald cross. "Never mind, I already know. In my dream, I was you, swimming in the sea, breathing easy. The sun was above and the sea grass moving in the water below. It was beautiful and peaceful. And then everything changed, its dark and I can't see. But I can see *her*. She wants it back. She pulled me to the deep by the necklace around my neck. *That* necklace. The chain tightened around my windpipe, and I couldn't breathe. There were bones on the bottom, bones of hundreds of people..... and... well, I woke up then. I swear I was covered in sea water."

Tears spilled down Ashley's face as she told the story. Clearly, she'd been affected by the dream. Chills raced up and down Lizzie's spine, her skin prickling. "Oh Lizzie, it scared me so much. I think something bad is going to happen to you, something with that wreck. It was a warning or something... I don't know."

Lizzie patted her friend's hand reassuringly. "It was just a dream. You know you must have jumbled things in your subconscious...."

"I *know* how these things work... You know everything I do is not a total sham! It was that necklace she pulled me down with. The woman was someone who reminded me of your mother, very disapproving. Something is up, something has changed for you, and it's not good. You should stay off that wreck at the very least. Have you still been trying to find information on Cami? You know I don't think that's a great idea, that Paul gives me the creeps..."

"Well, I won't be diving for a long time. I'm done out on the wreck and likely will never see Damen or another wetsuit for a very long time. Paul found some information, but nothing really to go on."

Ashley squeezed her hand. "You think maybe it might be time to let it go? At least until you can afford to have a *real* investigator?"

Lizzie sighed, bowing her head, suddenly tired, the evening a rollercoaster of drama starting with her mother's outburst. "You think I should stop looking for what happened to Cami?"

A rattling on a shelf full of candles and ornate bowls behind them got both women's attention. A glass bowl slipped off the shelf, crashing to the floor, its shards scattering over the tiles. "Your damn cat scares the daylights out of me, knocking things off shelves, giving me a heart attack," Lizzie said, her hand over her skipping heart. "I don't know how you put up with her."

Ashley looked at the wreckage on the floor, her mouth gaping open. "That's the thing Lizzie, it wasn't Sheba. My cat died this past winter."

Much later, Lizzie walked home alone, the night still steamy from the heat of the day. It was less than a mile from Ashley's house to hers, and the route was familiar. It was late, but she had no reason for concern. Tonight, the town was quiet, with most of the activity toward the downtown section.

She walked along, lost in her thoughts and what both Paul and Ashley had said. There was a lot to think about, and a lot of disappointment about the leads that came from Paul's information. A little detail, and then no more. Bits and pieces about Cami; speculation on the stolen care just raised more questions and wasn't likely connected. A familiar process throughout the entire investigation of Cami's disappearance.

Lizzie's fingers found the necklace as she thought about Ashley's dream. It was just like her to have something dramatic like that occur. It still chilled her, even though she knew it to be outrageous, typical Ashley.

She turned a corner to a quiet side street. The muted sound of footsteps sounded on the pavement behind her. A chill raced up her spine, putting her senses on alert. She shook it off, sure her reaction had to do with the influence of Ashley recounting her dream. There was no one in sight in front of her. She stopped walking and turned to see who was behind her. A figure darted from view, stepping onto a sidewalk leading to a cottage tucked into the live oaks that grew on either side of the dark street.

Her stomach trembled. It was likely someone who was staying in the house on the street, and she was just being paranoid. Turning back, she started walking toward home again, her senses on alert, listening to anyone else on the street with her. Her own pace quickened along with her heartbeat.

The sound of footsteps resumed behind her; her heart skipped in her chest. She continued walking for about half a block, trying to convince herself it was someone else walking down the street, and not the same person who had stepped off the sidewalk. But her own senses told her it was the same person.

She walked faster, and the footsteps increased to match her pace. Again, she whirled around, trying to catch whoever it was. The figure of a man concealed itself again. Now knowing it was not a kid out having fun scaring her, she became even more alarmed. Her parents' house was two blocks away. She could call for help, but she'd be home long before anyone came. Calling 911 would do the same, and what would she report? Hearing footsteps following her on the public street wasn't a crime.

This was scaring her. She couldn't lie to herself. A deep sense of foreboding shook her. Who was it that was following her?

Lizzie picked up her pace again, and the footsteps followed, keeping pace with her. Fear rose in her heart, and she ran, hearing the heavy footfalls behind her. She ran as fast as she could, her breath rasping in her chest at the sudden exertion and fear.

In several nerve-wracking moments, she finally reached her parents' house. Darting up the steps and fumbling with the old lock, she slipped into the quiet house, locking the door behind her. A car door slammed out front. She drew back the curtain and noticed a dimly lit vehicle quickly drive away from the opposite side of the street. It was too dark to make out the license plate numbers from where she stood.

She let out a deep sigh, urging her heart to calm its rapid thud in her chest. Her visit to Ashley had likely made her jumpy. This could have all been a coincidence, someone trying to get to their vehicle, but her gut told her otherwise.

Someone had been following her. *Who was it and what did they want?*

CHAPTER 15

Lizzie tossed and turned all night, sleeping fitfully. The change of environment back to her childhood room, the lack of the gentle rocking of the ocean, and all that had transpired since she had come back to shore kept her mind churning. Cami's case at the top of her mind. There was the matter of the additional DNA. Whose could it be? She hadn't asked the DNA source, not wanting to hear if she had been sexually assaulted. The possibility of rape and murder were likely, she knew. It was just hard to imagine.

Since she disappeared, there had never been a solid conclusion to what happened to her. There would be conjectures, thoughts, probabilities but never any solid evidence. The most solid was what they had found, her bathing suit with her DNA. Nothing else appeared in that location, if the police were really searching and knew what to look for. Lizzie threw her pillow on the floor in frustration. She may never know if they were taking the correct steps, whatever that may be, to locate evidence.

She always had a feeling the investigation hadn't been handled correctly, but she had no proof and nothing to gauge it by. It was likely that she would never know for certain unless she were to investigate herself or find someone to do it for her. Her parents would never approve of either, trusting completely in the law enforcement to do their jobs.

Lizzie understood Ashley's comment that Paul gave her the creeps. He was her only contact with the local law enforcement; the only person she had found willing to provide her with any information. Her mind went to the photo of the figure in the stolen car. She pulled it up on her phone where Paul had texted the information to her last night. There was something familiar about the shape of the head and the hair. It could be Cami, but it could also be anyone else. The capture of the driver was that poor. They intended for the bridge photo to capture the vehicle, and the license plate, not to identify the driver.

Paul had mentioned that the sheriff would be connecting with her parents in the next few days to reveal the official report on finding Cami's bathing suit. She was tied about sharing any information with them that would bring up the old wounds and pain of losing their daughter. However, they had a right to know of any tangible evidence, whether it provided any further information. Hopefully, they would come while she was still in town, and her father was with her mother. With both of them leaving to go back north, Lizzie for school, her father for work, her mother deserved some level of support. Whether she would accept it was the other question. She had her extended family present in the area; in case she needed additional support. It was doubtful her mother would accept emotional support from anyone, however.

A text from Marcus reminding her he'd be by to pick her up shortly shook her from the mire of her thoughts. The two cousins had a standing breakfast date when they were both in town. Marcus was an early riser, restless without Daniel around, would likely want to hang out with her all day. They had their last-minute packing and shipping to deal with, so it would be a busy day. Lizzie got out of bed and into the shower, grateful for the chores of packing to keep her mind off of the jumble of information received last evening.

Then there was the creepy incident of the person who had followed her from Ashley's. In the light of day, Lizzie wasn't entirely convinced that some of that was her own imagination. However, it had scared her, and she debated mentioning it to Marcus. He would definitely chalk it up to Ashley's influence; for that reason, she thought better of mentioning it.

As the water splashed over her in the shower, she thought of Damen. He was due out in the next few days as well, driving back to Norfolk. Remembering how his lips felt on hers... she hoped they'd run into each other just once more before they both finally left town. She couldn't get him out of her mind.

The sheriff's vehicle was in the driveway when Marcus dropped her off at her parent's later that morning. Lizzie took him up on his offer to join her in the support of her parents with the news of locating the bathing suit. The sheriff was just leaving as they joined them in the living room.

Lizzie's mother clutched a handkerchief in her hands. Her eyes were red rimmed. Her father escorted the sheriff to the door, thanking him. "Why do they tell us these things when they can't tell us where she is?" Soledad sobbed, rising from her chair angrily.

James reached out to console his wife, and she yanked her arm away from his touch, leaving the room with heavy footsteps. They all listened to her footfalls, waiting for the expected slamming of her mother's bedroom door. Lizzie sighed, not blaming her mother for her reaction to the news.

"Lizzie, they've located your sister's bathing suit in the dirt around the fort where some workers were digging. There's been no other evidence to suggest any crime was committed there, however it's been so long and with it being outdoors, they could be missing evidence." Lizzie's father reported, while gently touching her arm.

His tone was even and empathetic. She imagined him talking to his patients in the same manner while delivering bad news. "So, there's nothing else?" Lizzie asked, knowing full well of the answer already.

"No. Nothing concrete, and without.... Ah.. any further evidence of a crime, they don't know what happened," James replied, stepping delicately around mentioning the lack of body or remains of any kind.

"I see," Lizzie replied as James kissed her forehead. He would always protect her and be considerate of her feelings, unlike her mother. Neither of them showed any sign they knew she had the information before they did. It needed to stay that way, for now. Lizzie noted the difference in her parent's response, her father concerned for her. Her mother was concerned for herself. Nothing had changed.

The additional DNA, and the stolen vehicle had been left out of the conversation with her parents. On one hand, she was glad for it, on the other she wondered about the motive of the sheriff to withhold the inconclusive evidence and more from her parents.

Marcus turned the volume up on the TV that had been muted in the room's corner. "Did you see that they're saying we might get hit?" he said, referring to the hurricane's predicted path.

They all turned to watch the forecast, with the spaghetti models streaking across the maps on the screen. The storm had formed out in the Atlantic and was predicted to head to Cuba, but the models were predicting several paths, one with the Keys directly in the path. "We'll all be up north by the time it comes in here," her father said. "That is a big *if* they really don't know until it's much closer, anyway. It could miss us entirely, or even track up the East coast."

"We don't know until we know," Marcus agreed, snapping off the television.

Lizzie startled awake from a deep sleep, having finally drifted off around midnight. Was someone knocking? Her room was packed and ready for her to board their flight later that afternoon. Daniel was due in this morning and would have time to shower and change before heading to the airport. It was barely light out, so she hadn't overslept to meet Marcus for breakfast.

She reached out for her phone, noting several missed calls and texts from Marcus. She had left it in silent mode, hoping for a better night's sleep. A banging on the front door startled her. She felt a surge of adrenaline and her heart pounded. *Something was wrong.*

Lizzie bolted from her bed, careening down the stairs to answer the door. Her father was up and dressed, meeting her in the foyer. Whoever it was, the loud pounding reverberated off the thick door, shaking it on its hinges. James opened the door to Marcus on the steps, sobbing and wailing, his face contorted in panic. "Marcus, Marcus, what's happened? Are you hurt? Your parents?" Lizzie cried out.

James and Lizzie grabbed Marcus's arms to steady him as the young man stumbled across the threshold. "You've got to come with me, Lizzie. Down at the docks... there's been an accident... they sank... bringing survivors back now... I can't...."

"What ship sank?" Lizzie asked, trying to make sense of what he was saying. "There weren't any storms predicted last night. How could they have?.."

Marcus interrupted her, clutching at her arm. "It was the *Merchant* Lizzie. It sank last night. I'm not sure what happened... I was listening to the radio... Listen, do you hear the sirens?"

In the distance, they could hear the wail of sirens, a lot of them. Her blood ran cold.

"I'll bring you to the docks. Lizzie, you better put on some clothes," James said, taking over the situation with his distraught nephew.

In what seemed like hours, when it was only a few minutes, Lizzie found herself supported between her father and cousin standing at the docks. Several ambulances and police vehicles waited, their occupants stood looking out to sea, waiting silently.

The somber atmosphere chilled her. Further away, standing dockside at an empty berth, Lizzie could make out the figures of Isaac and Damen. The men stood apart, separated by rescue personnel. Isaac's shoulders slumped forward, appearing to be unsteady on his feet. Damen's broad back was to them, the stiffness in his posture clear to her as he watched a boat approach the docks.

Lizzie didn't recognize the ship. It was a fishing boat. Its deck full of people. As it docked, she saw several people with emergency blankets draped around their shoulders. She stepped forward to get a closer look, supported on both sides by her father and Marcus, who had calmed somewhat. His face remained full of anxiety.

Damen, Isaac and the rescue workers moved into action as soon as the boat docked, helping people to disembark, taking their arms, and moving them toward the waiting ambulances. As they drew nearer, Lizzie recognized the crew of the *Merchant*, but puzzled at their appearance. Their heads were covered in dark streaks of what appeared to be oil or diesel. She could smell it coming from people they passed.

Her feet felt leaden as she stepped forward, her eyes searching for Daniel in the crowd. Somber expressions found her. Someone reached out and squeezed her hand. She couldn't acknowledge any of it, couldn't absorb what was happening.

And then she stilled. Marcus froze at her side. Two rescue workers loaded a figure onto a stretcher covered in a sheet.

Time stood still.

Isaac approached the stretcher, with Damen at his side. The two men lifted the sheet from the prone figure's face.

Daniel.

In shock, Lizzie moved forward to see him, feeling she needed to be sure it was him. His blonde hair hung around his face with streaks of oily residue. Someone had wiped his face clean. He appeared to be sleeping, his expression peaceful and serene. How could this be?

Daniel.

Beside her, Marcus made a sound like a wounded animal sinking to his knees, pulling Lizzie to the ground with him. Grief and anguish filled her soul as she sobbed with her cousin.

Not my sweet Daniel. Oh, Daniel....

CHAPTER 16

Her fingers fumbled with the last buttons on her black blouse, feeling as though she were in a trance. The past few days were a bad dream she could not wake from. Down the hall, the clip of her mother's heels sounded on the tile floor. A knock at her door roused her from her daze. "Hija, are you ready? We must leave now to arrive with the family."

Her mother had found some of her maternal instincts and had been kind and supportive of her. She knew what it was like to lose someone close to her, aside from Cami, her mother's first husband had drowned at sea. Lizzie wasn't sure of all the details, but if it turned the frigid woman into a caring being for a moment, she'd take it. Such displays of affection from her mother were few in her life. Soledad's willingness to be with the Wisler's, made the situation easier. Notwithstanding it being the worst thing Lizzie had been through.

Of course, everyone thought of Lizzie as the grieving girl-friend. Marcus intended to leave the charade as it was, and not reveal his relationship with Daniel, at least not now, so soon after his death. It wasn't difficult; she had loved Daniel. Mourning him with his family was right. Marcus remained at her side, in his role as the best friend.

Lizzie clasped the emerald necklace around her neck, her thoughts moving to Ashley's dream. Some of it had come true, instead of it being her that drowned it had been Daniel. But it hadn't been the owner of the cross that pulled him to his death. It had been the malfunctioning bilge pumps. During the night, the ship took on water, while the crew slept, not noticing the ship listing to its side as it had in the storm last week. They'd all been awake then and were aware of the situation enough to rectify it quickly.

The sleeping crew and calm waters hadn't allowed for anytime to fix the damaged equipment and the water poured in unwitnessed. Weighed down by the silver bars and cannon the dive teams brought to the surface, the ship sank quickly.

Most of the crew had made it out, startled from their beds by the sudden shift of the ship, and water pouring into their quarters. Daniel had apparently made it out initially, only to dive back down to free a trapped crew member. He saved them but didn't make it out himself in time. Other crew members tried to save him, but it had been too late.

The crew tried their best to revive him, but as they had all been sleeping when it happened, no mayday had been called. No one knew they were in trouble and no help was on the way. Hours later, a fishing boat went by their location, noting the oil slick and flotsam from the sinking checked it out. The fisherman found the crew, floating in the sea, with one lifeboat and a dead crewmember. She shuddered to think about what the crew had gone through all night, knowing no help was on the way.

Kind and sweet Daniel was gone. A tear streaked down her cheek, and she took a deep breath, steeling herself for the event before her, and joined her parents to leave for the funeral home.

The services passed like a slow dream. The rituals of death, the kind words people whispered in her ears, passed by her like a fog. It was exhausting. It seemed hundreds of people from town, locals and friends joined them in the warm and cramped funeral home to say goodbye to Daniel. Many came because they knew the family or had worked for them, but most were friends of Daniel's.

Isaac had opted for an open casket, with the plan to have Daniel cremated after they completed the services. He had been too young to have made his wishes known, leaving Isaac to decide what was best for his son. Lizzie knew eventually they would spread his ashes on the ocean, where he had left them; and where he'd died saving someone else's life.

Near the end of the gathering, after the funeral service, Isaac approached Lizzie and Marcus, taking them both in his arms. "Thank you both for being such good friends with my Daniel. He loved you both very much."

New tears streaked down their faces. "We'll miss him so much," Lizzie could only whisper as her throat closed with new tears.

"You're family," Isaac said, clasping Lizzie's hand in his calloused grasp. "Please don't be a stranger. Stay in touch with an old man."

Lizzie hugged him back, with Marcus joining in. She vowed to do so. It would be the very least she could do to stay in touch with Daniel's grieving father. Isaac pulled back, looking into her face, his fingers finding the emerald cross around her neck. "Be sure to bring this to Damen for final cataloging. We need to have it appraised, and you can have it back afterward. Bring it to him before you go back north."

"Isn't he leaving too?" Lizzie asked, realizing he had to extend his leave for the services.

"Day after tomorrow, he's being deployed in a couple of weeks. You can catch him; you know the place?"

Lizzie nodded. She knew he'd been staying in a cabin near the salvage offices on Stock Island, if he wasn't in the office. It was near where they had docked the yacht, just a few days ago. "I'm going to be tied up prepping for the weather. We're going to have something from the hurricane, if it's not a direct hit," Isaac said, turning from the pair to speak to other visitors.

Damen flexed his fingers, concentrating on calming himself. There was nothing more he wanted to do in the world but to punch the man who sat next to him in the face. Not an appropriate action to take while at his little brother's funeral, smashing the grieving father's face with his fist.

That they were at Daniel's funeral was his father's fault. It was his willing neglect of the equipment that led to the ship sinking. Yes, they had been able to jerry-rig the gear to get it to work, and it had been successful. But his one time it hadn't, with the pumps quitting as the crew slept in their bunks. And now Daniel was dead. Had Isaac done what he originally said he would, bringing the *Viking* out a few days ago, and bringing the *Merchant* back for repairs, his brother would still be alive.

Rage pulsed in his veins. He knew it was a self-protective mechanism to allow the anger to take over his emotions, not permitting the grief in. He was very familiar with the ability to do this, having lost team members on engagements from a bullet or a bomb and needing to continue on with the mission at hand. For another time, he pushed away those emotions. They would come to the surface when he least expected, but they would come back. That he knew well.

This time his mission was to finish what he started while on leave, helping his father out, wrap up paperwork, pack up and leave. He never intended to return. There was nothing left for him here. He could barely stand to look at Isaac.

Damn his father, damn the salvage business and damn the treasure. He never wanted it, and now it was tainted with his brother's life. Damen knew his path was back with his teammates, his brothers in arms. It was the life that he chose, and that chose him. He was good at it, the dangerous life of keeping the world safe. It would be his life's work, not looking for trinkets at the bottom of the sea.

Damen's eyes followed Lizzie as the mourners offered her their condolences. He couldn't help himself, drawn to her as he was. Daniel's girl. She raised her red-rimmed eyes, catching him staring at her. He held the gaze instead of turning away, a jolt of lust socking him squarely in the gut.

Another thing to not be thinking at his brother's funeral, unfinished business with his dead brother's girl. He pushed the thoughts from his mind, and the complications that a relationship would bring into his life. It would be business that would remain unfinished.

CHAPTER 17

She moved through the days as if in a daze, walking through mud. Lizzie went through the motions of getting ready for school, trying to get Marcus to take part in preparing. Classes were already in session, and she wasn't sure she could handle the school year, but she had to. It was too late to get a refund on her courses, and she needed to complete her coursework to get into medical school. Any gaps would delay her and even put her future in jeopardy.

James had reminded her of this, gently at first, permitting her space to absorb the shock of losing Daniel. But her father would not permit this tragedy to ruin her life and was now firmly guiding her to go back and return to her studies. The routine of the classes and work would help her heal, keeping her mind elsewhere.

Marcus was not so lucky to have a parent engaged in his life guiding him forward. Attending college had been more the promise of a life outside of home for him with Daniel. And now he was gone. Marcus was despondent in his grief. His ambition had left, and it was doubtful he would put effort into finishing school. Marcus's family was indifferent to whether or not he completed his studies. They had their wealth, and he had his trust fund to rely on. He didn't need to work if he didn't want to.

Lizzie had rearranged their flights and took care of contacting the school, intercepting the packages they had mailed, and all the things that Marcus would have been on top of. Now he didn't care what happened.

James advised Lizzie to monitor Marcus, concerned he was heading into a clinical depression. As his uncle, he cared about the young man. Lizzie knew James would check in on him and her while they were at school. It was comforting to know he would be around as always. James would fly up with them. Lizzie knew he wanted to be sure they settled in and were managing without their best friend. He would also make sure she returned to her studies; she knew. It was going to be a tough year without Daniel in the apartment.

Lizzie caught her reflection in her bedroom mirror, the emerald necklace she still wore around her neck glinting in the light. She needed to return it to the salvage company, which meant she would be required to see Damen again, if only for a few moments to take care of the transaction. The thought was both intimidating and appealing. Even through all the events of the past few days, she still thought of his lips on hers, his hands on her body. She felt a wave of electricity course through her body as the thought crossed her mind. It was too soon for Daniel's girlfriend to be interested in another man, but she really wasn't Daniel's girl. The charade was over.

No one was around for her to catch a ride to the salvage company offices, so Lizzie opted to take an Uber. Her driver was talkative and friendly, dropping her off from the quick ride outside the offices on Stock Island near the docks. Damen's truck was parked in the lot, which meant he was around, either in the offices or in the small cabin he slept in while home. She hoped it was in the offices, limiting any chance of a personal interaction with others around wanting to both see him and avoid seeing him at the same time.

The door to the offices was locked, and the lights were off inside. A note on the door instructed anyone with urgent business to go around back to Damen's cabin. It was likely that the crew were engaged in prepping for the impending hurricane. As of this morning, they predicted the hurricane was heading to Cuba, but it was a large storm and would cause high winds and water for the Keys. Any turn to the path would bring the storm their way.

Lizzie had half paid attention to the news on the hurricane, knowing she would be gone from the area before it was supposed to hit. Their flight was still on time and there had been no change to their itinerary. They would get out in time.

She followed the worn dirt path to a row of tiny cabins, built a long time ago to house sailors and crew of the ships that came into dock for repairs. The buildings had a weathered look to them, but the grass was neatly trimmed and the shrubs and plants gave the space a vibrant feel. Daniel had mentioned they would often have guests stay here, rather than in their cramped home, which was more a bachelor pad for Isaac and his sons as they came and went.

The salvage company had many investors and business dealings to support their continued search for treasure. The construct of the business was mind-boggling, with the taxes and issues with the government seizing treasure or claiming part of what they found. Isaac would be on his own with it until he sold or closed the business altogether. Now that neither of his children were to follow in his footsteps. Lizzie wondered what would become of him, the business and the treasure. She'd vowed to stay in touch with the man, so likely she'd find out.

The little sitting porch creaked under her feet as she stepped up to the door, painted a cheery yellow to match the Bahamian theme of the row of cabins. Her knuckles sounded on the wood, her heart rising in her throat from nerves as she silently wished no one was at home. Hesitating, she knocked a second time, harder and louder than the first. The door opened, yanked back from her hand as she knocked. "What do you .... Oh," Damen said, apparently surprised to find her on his doorstep. "Hello."

Lizzie stepped back, feeling a tightness in her throat. Damen stood shirtless, his boxer shorts falling loosely around his hips. His enormous arms and muscled chest were bare as he leaned on the doorframe, his size both intimidating and intriguing. A smattering of tattoos across his skin made him look even more menacing. She was used to seeing him dressed casually, with a bathing suit or shorts on, when they were working together on the dive boat. There was something different now, something both dangerous and sexy. Lizzie couldn't find her voice.

"To what do I owe the pleasure?" he asked casually.

Lizzie noted his eyes were red rimmed, his short hair ruffled, and he was unshaven. "I'm sorry. Did I wake you?" she said, stumbling over her words.

Damen huffed. "No. I've been up for hours, just haven't showered yet," he looked her up and down. "Come in, come in. We're letting all the cool air out."

Damen gestured for her to enter the small cabin, and she hesitantly stepped inside, her eyes adjusting to the dim light. The cabin was serviceable, with an open living room and a galley kitchen. A door in the back of the room was open, revealing a bedroom. She imagined a bath off of the bedroom. It was adequate for one person to stay and be able to spread out. A definite improvement over a hotel room, but not a home. Since Damen spent most of his time on leave on the *Merchant* or with her on the yacht, it was decent enough accommodation for the few days he stayed in town.

Damen excused himself briefly to the bedroom. While she waited, Lizzie settled on the miniature couch and surveyed her surroundings. The kitchen table was covered in paperwork and had a cup of barely touched coffee on it. A bottle of bourbon, only half full, sat on the counter, and Damen's belongings were piled up in the corner of the cramped living room. It looked as though he was packed and ready to leave.

He emerged fully dressed in shorts and a formfitting black t-shirt from the bedroom. "Can I offer you anything to drink? Coffee, water? I know you don't like bourbon...."

"No thank you," she replied, nervously shifting on the small couch.

He joined her sitting beside her, the only other seating aside from the metal kitchen chairs. "What can I do for you?" he asked kindly, his gaze filled with caution.

"Isaac asked that I drop the necklace by, to you directly before I left," she said, nervously stumbling over her words.

Damen frowned; his face puzzled. "Ahh, I see. No one's in the office?"

Lizzie shook her head, reaching up to finger the delicate chain around her neck. "No, the door's locked, lights off. A note on the door says to come back here."

Damen shrugged. "Ah, I see"

"Isaac said he'd be busy getting ready for the storm."

Damen shrugged his shoulders, shaking his head. "Getting ready down at Captain Tony's, I assume."

He shook his head at her confused expression, brushing it off. "Never mind, no worries. I'll make sure the necklace gets to the right place."

Lizzie reached behind her head to unclasp the necklace, nervously fumbling with the clasp, unable to make it work. Her fingers feeling clumsy, unable to unlock the mechanism releasing the necklace. Damen watched her struggle and scooted closer to her to help with the clasp at the back of her neck. His fingertips made her skin tingle as he worked the ancient clasp. She could feel his breath in her hair.

"Boy, they meant this to not slip off easily," Damen muttered.

Lizzie felt his fingers jerk with the chain releasing. "There" he exclaimed.

He brought his hands over her head, releasing the jewelry. The chain and cross skimming her breasts as he lifted it, his eyes following the movement. Clearing his throat, he rose abruptly from the couch, busying himself with the papers on the small table, riffling until he located an envelope, slipping the necklace inside. "I'll log it and bring it to the safe in the office later and I'll leave instructions for Alice to send it to you at school if that's what you want, or drop it off at your mother's?"

"Thank you. Either would be fine, whatever is most convenient," Lizzie answered, her gaze following his movements.

Damen moved back to the couch. "It may be best to leave it with your mother, particularly if it's as valuable as I think it will be. Safer than sending it through the mail or a courier," he said, reaching out to touch her hand. "How are you?"

Lizzie sighed. "I still can't believe it happened. I miss him so much," she replied. "And you?"

"Same. It shouldn't have happened," Damen growled.

"I know you're angry with your father, but he's grieving, too."

"I hope he rots in hell."

Lizzie knew the relationship was strained between the two men, but the accident was the last straw for Damen. He blamed Isaac for his stinginess, not putting money into the ship, and not bringing the *Viking* out sooner.

"You're leaving?" she asked, motioning to the bags in the corner.

"Yeah, tomorrow morning, early. I have to report back. It's a long drive to Norfolk."

"Isaac mentioned you were being deployed soon. How long will you be gone?"

"From here? Forever, I'm not coming back. There is no reason to now. Daniel was the only family I had left."

Lizzie shifted uneasily at the icy anger in his voice, knowing any further plea for him to stay in touch with his father would fall on deaf ears. He'd made his mind up. "I meant for the deployment. How long will you be away?"

"Twelve weeks."

"Do you know where you're headed?"

Damen shook his head. "It's classified."

They sat in an uncomfortable silence, Lizzie wanting to say something more. They had bonded so well at the dive site, but they were both leaving tomorrow, and it seemed unlikely they'd ever see each other again. With a feeling of resignation, she arose to her feet. He followed her.

"Well, I guess I'll be going. Thanks for your help with the necklace," she said, reaching out to embrace him. He stiffly accepted her touch as she gently kissed his cheek. His hands moved to her shoulders, as he returned the gesture, his beard grazing her cheek, sending a shiver down her spine, her skin erupting in gooseflesh.

He froze, his lips still on her cheek. Lizzie took a sharp intake of air, as an immediate fire burned in her belly.

"Lizzie," he whispered, his voice gravel.

He pulled her into his arms, and she felt the subtle whisper of his breath against her neck as his lips left a trail of fire. His immediate effect on her was dizzying. She could feel her heart thumping wildly in her chest. "Damen." She softly whispered his name.

His hands roved her body, moving up and down her back, over her buttocks, clasping her hips and pulling her into his arousal. His mouth met hers, their lips parting as he kissed her passionately. "What you do to me," he murmured, "I want you, Lizzie, and this time there's no holding back."

He gripped her shoulders, pushing her back gently to look into her face. His gaze was intense and burning. "Do you want this? You need to know there is no future. After tomorrow, we both go our separate ways."

She stilled. She knew this, deep down. If she gave in to her desire and slept with him, it would not mean he loved her. It may be a high price to pay for her desire. However, no man had made her feel the way he did. The flare of passion in her belly was incomparable. The way her body responded to his touch had never happened with another man. In the back of her mind, she knew under his coarse exterior that he was a kind man, having seen glimpses during their time on the dive boat. She wanted to believe, despite the odds against them, that there was love for her in him. She could sense the embers within her own heart, as well as an intense desire that was almost unbearable.

Keeping her eyes on his face, Lizzie stepped back, causing him to drop his hands to his sides. Slowly, she unbuttoned her blouse; the fabric slipping from her shoulders and onto the floor. She reached to the straps of her bra, slipping them from her shoulders. He stepped forward, stilling her hands under his. "Let me," he whispered, his breath hitching in his throat.

Slowly, he slipped the straps from her shoulders, reaching behind and releasing the catch in one swift move. His hands found her breasts, naked in his rough skin. Her nipples hardened under his touch, and his eyes darkened with passion.

He swept her up in his arms, cradling her body close as he carried her to the bedroom and laid her gently down on the bed. He slowly peeled off his shirt before he lowered himself onto her, his lips finding hers, and slowly skating down her neck to her breasts. She moaned under his touch. "You're so beautiful. I've wanted this for so long," he whispered.

His hands unclasped her shorts, pushing them down while his hand found her silky heat. She nearly came with his touch. Eager now, she pulled at his shorts, unclasping them. They hastened to remove their clothes, their bodies eagerly drawn to each other as soon as they were free of fabric.

Lizzie felt her body burn with unbridled passion, as an urgent need consumed her. "I need you now," she moaned under him, unable to contain herself.

In one move he entered her, and she caught her breath at the size of him as he filled her gently at first, his hips moving slowly over her. She pulled him deeper still into her, wrapping her legs around his, thrusting herself into him as their rhythm grew.

A strong current of heat surged between them, the intensity of their passion and need growing as they moved together in perfect rhythm. She shouted his name as her body shuddered. His thrusts grew urgent and then he cried out in passion, joining her ecstasy as he collapsed, spent on the pillows beneath her.

CHAPTER 18

The late afternoon light fell across their tangled bodies on the bed in the tiny cabin. Damen twirled a strand of Lizzie's hair between his fingers, watching her face as she dozed in his arms. Just this morning, he'd been a free agent, a single man with no responsibilities to anyone. Sleeping with her had been a mistake. It had opened something deep inside of him, the tight box of emotion he'd kept a firm handle on for the past 30 years. There was no lying to himself, no way he could take what she'd opened in his heart and shove it back down inside where it belonged.

It terrified him.

He had a career of being one of the most dangerous men on the planet, handling terrorists, radicals threatening the country on covert missions; the details of which he couldn't share with anyone. Handling the insane was his life's work. Handling, falling in love with his dead brother's girl, shook his core.

He was taken by surprise. This was something he was not expecting, nor had any room for in his life. It also wasn't practical. They were both headed in opposite directions in life, physically separated. She wouldn't fit into his life, especially since he'd leave for parts unknown and be gone for a protracted time. Experiencing a relationship with a special forces member was like having a relationship with a ghost. Gone for lengths of time to undisclosed locations for unknown amounts of time took its toll on family relationships. He'd seen some make it, staying together with families and marriages. But he'd seen more failure than success. It would be unfair to her to ask for a long-distance relationship, doomed before it even got off the ground.

What was he thinking? Damen knew himself well enough to know. He had no control over his desire for her. It had consumed him, his need to touch her, possess her.

She'd just lost Daniel, they both had. Lizzie was still tender and would be for a while. Likely he was the closest thing she could get to replacing his brother. He pushed the thought aside; she'd responded to him when they were on the yacht together, and Daniel was still alive. She wanted *him*, not a dead man.

Her eyelids fluttered, and she opened her eyes, looking into his face. She shifted her body to face him, smiling sexily. He felt his body respond to the movement, and he held himself still. "Hey there," she purred, cuddling her naked form against his hardness.

He wrapped his arms around her, pulling her closer. "Hi beautiful," he whispered. "I've been thinking... maybe I was a little abrupt. You know what I said earlier, that there was no future ... with me."

Her brown eyes were cautious as he continued. "I meant.... I'm gone a lot... I have a dangerous job. A relationship is just not possible, long distance and all."

She stilled in his arms. "Right, not the best situation.... But wait... am I hearing a change of heart? Are you saying you would want to... if the circumstances were different?"

His breath stilled as his heart rate climbed. "I'm not willing to change the *situation....*"

"It's who you are," she said, agreeing, using his own words.

"We could try. The odds would be against us... but if you wanted... I'd be game to see where this takes us."

Lizzie slid herself on top of him, her silky skin brushing over his body, making the fire light where her skin touched his. She kissed him, her breasts crushing into his chest, her tongue joining with his. "I'd like that," she whispered, pulling back from the kiss, smiling widely.

She shifted, taking him inside of her. They both moaned in unison as he filled her. He felt his heart shift as new emotions rose to the surface. This may be a mistake and not end well. But right now, he was willing to try with the gorgeous woman straddling him.

Sometime later, the shadows lengthened in the tiny bedroom. It was late afternoon, and they both needed to get back to prepping to leave in the morning. A loud and jolting alarm disrupted the peaceful atmosphere. Both their phones were going off with a loud and obnoxious alert. They scurried from the bed, locating their cells in the clothing tossed on the floor. "What the hell is happening?" Lizzie swore, stumbling around the room, finally locating her phone.

"A mandatory evacuation has been ordered," Damen said, heading to the outer room while pulling on his shorts.

He switched on the small television in the living area, bringing up the local channels. "They've issued mandatory evacuations for the Florida Keys, as the hurricane Irma is now bearing down on them. She's expected to come on shore as a high Category 4 storm with winds over 182 miles an hour, and storm surges of 8 feet or more. Folks, this is the real deal. A storm of this magnitude is not survivable. If you stay, you will be underwater. You need to be making plans now to leave."

Damen's blood ran cold. They'd been through some dreadful storms over the years. Something like this wasn't like anything he remembered. "I guess it's a good thing we're leaving tomorrow. Check on your flight. Make sure it's not canceled because of the weather."

Lizzie was already checking in on the details of her flight on her phone. "My mother, I have to go home and see if she's going to go. She'll need to leave, too." Lizzie scooted around the room, picking up her clothing and dressing quickly. "Can you give me a lift?"

"I doubt my old man will leave. The natives can be pretty stubborn and foolish," Damen said, gathering his shirt and keys.

Before they stepped out the door of the cabin, Damen pulled Lizzie into his arms. "I meant what I said. I know you're going through a lot, losing my brother. But I don't want to lose touch with you, let's see where this takes us."

Smiling, she kissed him. "I want that too."

Warmed with the possibilities, a little afraid of the new emotions rising in him, he took her hand and left the cabin, locking the door behind them.

CHAPTER 19

Lizzie's heart soared as Damen kissed her before letting her out of his truck outside her parent's. The past few hours seemed like a dream. Never before had she felt this way about anyone. She turned to wave goodbye to him, giddy with the emotions that bubbled up inside. Damen waved back, smiling broadly. While their lives were taking them in different directions, she was hopeful to explore where this attraction took them. They'd made plans to connect in the morning, after making sure their families had plans to weather the storm.

As she walked up the front path, the door to her parent's home opened. Her father stood in the doorway, his face unreadable. Guilt immediately rose in her gut. She was supposed to be in mourning for losing her boyfriend, as the world saw her. She shouldn't be excited to be beginning a relationship with his brother. Had James seen them kiss in front of the house? What was he thinking of her now?

The air left her lungs and her feet felt like they were walking in cement in the few steps it took to reach her father. His lips were tight in his face, his eyes lined with stress. "You've heard of the evacuation order?" he asked. "Your mother is refusing to leave."

Lizzie took a deep breath, relieved that James's reaction wasn't about Damen. As she had expected, her mother was going to be difficult with the hurricane warnings. "Are you surprised?" she mumbled, moving past her father into the house. "She wouldn't go to a shelter either, will she?"

"Can you try to convince her? I've tried," he said, his voice revealing that he was on his last nerve.

This may be that last straw in their relationship that Lizzie had been expecting, she realized. While their breakup was expected, its reality pulled at her heartstrings. Her family was unraveling. No matter what age a child is at, it matters when their parents split apart. Tears welled in her eyes. She blinked them away before her father saw them.

"I'll try, but you know how she is. I'll call Marcus to help. It'll take his mind off of Daniel for a little while at least."

Lizzie caught the expression on her father's face, the agreement and question mingling together. *He knows...* she thought, before he turned away. "That sounds like a good idea. Give him something else to focus on. She listens to him," he replied. "Was that Daniel's brother who dropped you off?"

Lizzie didn't meet her father's gaze and turned to head up the stairs to her room. "Isaac needed the necklace back before I went north. He asked that I drop it by their offices on Stock Island to Damen. It needs to be appraised and catalogued with the rest of the treasure before he can distribute anything to the crew."

"That's quite generous. It has to be quite a valuable piece."

"I didn't know this before volunteering to help, but it's part of how they compensate the divers who've helped to find and recover the treasure. They give a portion of the money to the divers, as well as pay for the time on the dive."

This intrigued her father, and he turned back to her, full of questions. "I'd like to hear more about it. It really sounds fascinating. We can chat on the flight tomorrow. But now please help me with your mother..."

Lizzie nodded, taking the stairs two at a time to her room, eager to connect with Marcus and get away from her father. He always seemed to know too much about what she was doing. If she had to swear to it, she was certain by his expression that he *knew* about the true nature of Marcus and Daniel's relationship. As she considered this tidbit, a realization dawned on her. James had been so strict with her about her studies and having her avoid distractions to concentrate on her future, but he had never objected to her relationship with Daniel. He'd never once tried to influence her to focus on her career over Daniel, and she was *living* with him while they were at school.

She'd been blind to her father's knowledge of their ruse. It was obvious. Had she been in love with Daniel, as his girlfriend, James would most certainly have addressed it with her. There would be no way that she wouldn't have heard some warning. Did other people realize this?

She sighed. Daniel was gone, her heart pained over the loss of her friend. She would never forget him. Now he was gone, their fake relationship was gone with him, and it was Marcus suffering now as she would have had their relationship been amorous. There was no need to address her father's probable knowledge of their cover with him, or anyone now. It no longer mattered. Marcus would come out when he was ready. All Lizzie could do was to love him and support him.

It would be interesting to see how her father responded to her budding relationship with Damen. Lizzie moved her fingers to her lips, recalling their passion just a short time ago. She wanted to see where life would take them if it would work out between them. He'd awakened something in her she'd never felt for any other man. It both scared her and made her want more.

She dialed Marcus's phone, glad to give him something to focus on before they left tomorrow. They needed his help to convince her mother to leave, and she wanted to talk with him, unsure if she would share her new potential for a relationship with Damen. Daniel's death had broken his heart. He needed her love and support more than anything now.

CHAPTER 20

Damen whistled to himself, taking the short drive back to the Stock Island offices, his thoughts on Lizzie. He knew that a relationship would not be a piece of cake, and was already in a precarious situation, but he was content that he was taking the risk. Having any kind of relationship with him would be hard, but that also applied to Lizzie. She would be in medical school, studying hard, doing early morning and late-night rotations to get her clinical in. There would be residencies and then working her way through specialties as he father wanted her to be a surgeon.

Was he crazy to consider this at all? If the past weeks had been a testament to making sure life had meaning, this was it. Life was short. He knew that from the work he did and losing his brother. Daniel had his life ahead of him, and in an instant, it was gone. His future and Lizzie's impacted forever.

Doubt crept into his thoughts again. Was he crazy to consider a relationship with a woman who had just lost her long-time boyfriend, who was his brother? When he looked at it like that, it made little sense. She was grieving. They both were. How could they even think this would have a chance?

He sighed, stopping at a traffic light before turning into the docks where the offices and cabins were. They'd see. That was all he could say. His gut kept telling him it was the right thing to stay connected to her, and his gut kept him alive while he was in the field. There was something more than just an attraction. He *knew* there was he felt it in his heart.

The relationship statistics he knew of his peers rose in his mind. He pushed them away. It was possible.

As he pulled into the dockyards, he saw police cruisers with their lights flashing parked outside the salvage offices. What had happened? He hadn't been gone that long, just leaving for maybe 30 minutes to bring Lizzie home. Alice, the long-time office manager, stood by talking to the police. Alarms inside the building were blaring, the front window of the salvage offices broken in pieces. Broken glass everywhere.

Damen's heart leaped in his throat. The large safe they'd been stashing the smaller items from the treasure was in this office. They'd loaded the bars of silver and gold into the maritime museum downtown that had 24/7 security. There was no security here, just the alarms system that was now blaring. Because of the hurricane preparations, the office staff here had been busy. The office was unattended. Damen had just left the area to bring Lizzie home. Leaving moments for someone to rob the office.

This was insane for there to be a break in here in broad daylight. The docks were already bustling with activity as boats were being prepped to survive the storm or lifted from the water entirely.

He quickly parked and joined the conversation with Alice and the police officer. "What's happened?" he asked, approaching the pair.

"You father is on his way over. I was just coming back when I got the alarm on my phone. Someone broke in, Damen. They broke into the safe," Alice said, wringing her bony hands together. "The police were here when I got here."

Damen recognized one officer to be the young deputy that Lizzie had spoken to at the hospital when they were waiting for Daniel. It seemed like a lifetime ago that Daniel was still alive.

Both officers were eying him suspiciously, making Damen's internal alarm sound. Something wasn't right about how they were looking at him. One had his hand on his sidearm, as though ready to draw. "What's going on?" he asked, calming his voice to diffuse the situation as tensions rose.

"Where were you just now?" the shorter man asked, approaching Damen cautiously.

He knew he could take out both youngsters within seconds, even though he wasn't armed. They would be no challenge to him. He hoped they didn't try anything foolish; he stilled himself to remain calm and find out what was causing them to look at him with suspicion.

"I was downtown, bringing a friend home," he answered, keeping his voice calm. "Have we been robbed?"

"They took everything in the safe, and they wrote on the walls. Vandals, I don't know what this world in coming too!" Alice interjected; her cigarette laced voice grating through the tension.

Damen moved slowly toward the office door, both officers heeling him. "I need to ask you to step over here. That's a crime scene."

He continued his forward motion, drawn to the broken office window. The items in the safe were valuable. They hadn't yet all been appraised or reported. The work was half done on them; guilt rose in his gut. He'd been slow to help his father in the past days, angry with him over Daniel's death. They wouldn't be able to claim everything that had been stolen, unless the archeologist kept good records. Damen knew that he did. It may be their saving grace.

As he looked through the broken window, his breath caught in his throat. The scent of fresh paint assaulted his senses, coupling with the still blaring alarm. They had trashed the office, papers were strewn everywhere, ripped and crumpled and scattered over the desks and the floor. The safe in the back of the room was wide open, empty cartons and other packing debris scattered everywhere. They had cleaned them out. The portion of the treasure that had been stored here was gone.

But what took his attention more than the missing treasure were the words painted in red paint scrawled on the wall.

Murderer!

Damen Wisler killed Cami Legard

His blood ran cold, and he swore loudly. "What the hell is this?"

Both officers flanked him. "Sir, we'd like to ask you some questions!"

"Hold on a minute, did you check my cabin?" he asked, turning from the men to hustle down the short walkway to the cabins in the back of the building. They trailed after him, yelling for him to halt. He proceeded, needing to find out if the robbery had affected his temporary residence.

The door was ajar, but he moved ahead, wanting to find out what they'd taken. When he stepped in the doorway, he paused. His cabin was completely ruined, his things were tossed around the area, and they ripped the papers he was working on to pieces. Damen's gaze roved the table and floor in search of the envelope in which he'd left Lizzie's necklace. The sight of the cabin's destruction made his stomach churn. He couldn't find the envelope.

It was gone. They'd taken the necklace. Who could have done this? Their security was decent enough, likely less than it really should have been considering the treasure they'd just found. But what about the accusation on the wall? What the hell was that about? Someone was accusing him of murder?

A firm hand touched his arm. "We have a few questions for you, sir. If you would please come with us down to the station."

Damen pulled back from the hand on his arm. "Are you arresting me?"

"No sir, we just have some questions." The young deputy took his arm. This time Damen complied. He'd need his attorney, and his commanding officer would need to be notified. He didn't have time for this BS, but it looked like he'd need to. It was unbelievable that they were taking the claim seriously.

Damen allowed the officers to lead him back to the front of the office, to the cruisers parked outside. His father's truck was parked crookedly next to his. He recognized the figure of his father peering through the broken window of the offices. The alarm was now, thankfully, silenced.

"Hey what's this?" Isaac demanded, coming to Damen's side. "You can't be serious; you can't arrest somebody for crazy graffiti...."

"We're just taking him down to the station for questioning, sir. That's all." The young deputy, Lizzie's friend, replied seriously, opening the back door of the cruiser for Damen.

"That's foolish. I'm calling the sheriff!" Isaac shouted as Damen slipped into the back of the cruiser.

"Call a lawyer, Dad. Have him meet me at the station."

Isaac's face reddened with the situation, his face an expression of disbelief. "I'll meet you down there son, we'll put an end to this nonsense. I've just been robbed for goodness' sakes! Don't say anything until Alex gets there, son."

The door slammed next to him. Great, Alex was one of his father's longtime drinking buddies. Damen hoped he knew what he was doing.

Damen's head was pounding. He'd been held in the tiny interview room in the Key West Sheriff's department for hours. So far, he'd been questioned once, and since his lawyer still needed time to sober up, he'd not answered questions. The situation concerned him; he needed to leave before sunrise to make it back to base on time. The mandatory evacuation meant that it would clog the roads with everyone else that was leaving to get out of the hurricane's path. Traffic would be at a standstill, making it entirely possible that he would be late. Damen needed to contact his commanding officer, both to report the situation he was in, and to let him know he'd be late. Neither piece of news would be well received.

As he was not being officially arrested, he could call his CO, while being observed by yet another deputy. Damen was right in the response from his boss. He wasn't happy with the situation. "The other compounding factor to this situation, Wisler, is that we have moved your deployment up. We need you back on base ASAP. The team needs you. They'll be wheels up tomorrow after the briefing 0800."

Damen winced at his words. He was normally eager to operate and do his duty, but he wanted to connect with Lizzie before they deployed him. At this rate, it would doom their relationship before it had even really begun.

From what he could gather from their line of questioning, the police were not interested in the robbery. They were asking him about where he was the day Lizzie's sister Cami went missing eight years ago! The whole situation perplexed him. There had to be something more they weren't telling him, something about the message on the wall accusing him of murder.

He wasn't guilty of any crime, and he hoped that there wasn't any question of his innocence. He settled himself in his seat. The situation was now in the hands of his commanding officer, and he knew the Navy would be involved with one of its own.

CHAPTER 21

S oledad had finally agreed to evacuate after a lengthy session of convincing, with Marcus at the helm of the discussion. He'd been in his element, persuading his aunt to leave and do as the authorities bid for her safety. The four of them were enjoying cocktails together, finally relaxing with their plans made to leave in the early morning.

Her mother would fly out with her brother, Marcus's father, on his private jet. They would stay inland in Miami with some of their extended family. The hurricane was not supposed to directly impact the Miami area, so they would be out of its path. Soledad had been reluctant to agree to go farther north, claiming it was too cold. Lizzie knew the truth in her reluctance. In case Cami showed up, she didn't want to stray far from home.

Lizzie hoped her mother knew that the possibility was likely out of the question. After all, she'd been told this many times. But still her mother's heart hoped, and Lizzie wondered if it had been her; would she have waited for her the same as she continued to do for Cami?

"I'm going up to bed," her mother announced, obviously worn down from the convincing her family had done. That and several martinis, Lizzie thought, glad the discussion had ended well. They'd all be off in the morning, out of harm's way.

Her thoughts shifted to Damen; she'd thought they would have a moment at least to say goodbye before they both left. But he wasn't answering her texts, and her call went straight to voicemail.

A knock on the front door startled her from her thoughts. Her father rising to answer the door. "It's late to have any visitors," he said.

"I hope they don't wake your mother. That was rough Lizzie," Marcus said, slipping onto the couch beside her.

She kissed his cheek. "You're wonderful with her. She listens to you. Unlike the rest of us…" She stopped talking at Marcus's expression of surprise and alarm.

The sheriff entered the living room, closely followed by her father. "Apologies for the late hour, I wanted to talk with you all before you left. There's been a development."

Lizzie's stomach dropped, and Marcus grasped her hand. "Certainly, if you don't mind keeping voices down, Soledad is sleeping," James said, quietly closing the living room doors behind him.

The sheriff raised his eyebrows at his old friend. "She may be interested in what I have to say."

"I'll relay the information to her. Tonight has been… a challenge…"

"If you say so, James." The big man took a seat in front of the couch, where James joined Marcus and Lizzie. "Later this afternoon, there was a robbery at the Wisler Salvage offices. The perpetrators cleaned out the safe. They got anything of value in the office and in the cabin in the back, where Damen Wisler was staying."

Lizzie's stomach lurched, *Damen*! Her hand flew to her neck. The necklace! Had they gotten that? "Is he all right?" she asked.

The sheriff studied her face. "No one was injured. It occurred while both buildings were unoccupied. If you're referring to the younger Mr. Wisler, he's in custody right now at the station."

"What? Why?" Lizzie cried out; Marcus squeezed her hand.

"That's why I'm here, little lady. The perpetrators left a message painted on the wall, and some evidence leading us to dig a little deeper." The older man reached into his pocket and pulled out a photo, handing it to James. "Someone believes Damen Wisler had something to do with Cami's disappearance."

Her father's face blanched at the photo; Lizzie leaned forward to look at it with Marcus. Seeing the message spelled out in red dripping letters. "Is that...?" Marcus whispered.

"It's red paint."

"You can't think he did anything.... From someone who'd break in?" Lizzie asked incredulously.

"No, little lady, we don't. However, there was an object left at the scene, a potential murder weapon, that we're sending out for testing. It seems like the younger Mr. Wisler is of some importance to the Navy. They're sending him back tonight. His CO has already called me twice, their sending MPs over to retrieve him, making sure he's going. He's hitching a ride out from the base here. They're all evacuating." The sheriff relayed this dump of information with no response to the shocked faces around him.

Lizzie felt the room spin; bile rose in her throat. *Damen kill Cami? What had they found? Surely it couldn't be.*

"Wasn't he among the group of men and boys questioned when she first disappeared?" James asked, remaining calm. "It doesn't make sense to pull him in now. Isaac Wisler has as many enemies as he does friends. It seems very opportunistic to me." James frowned disapprovingly at the sheriff.

"What did they find?" Marcus asked, leaning forward on the couch.

The sheriff looked sharply at Marcus, his brows furrowing. "At this point, we're keeping that under wraps. As we found nothing else at the site where her suit was found, we closed that up. I've got complaints from a Park Ranger that someone was digging on the property earlier today. I'm putting two and two together here, but until I have something solid, we're no closer to finding out what happened. It won't change the outcome, but it would give us a chance to close the case and give you all some closure."

He stood and looked down at them sitting on the couch. "The trouble is, we've got a hurricane headed for us, and I don't have the resources to dedicate to investigating right now. They're predicting the storm surge to put the beach and park under a few feet of water. I'd say they did the robbery when they knew people would be otherwise occupied, and I would focus the police on saving lives rather than looking for stolen property."

They all rose and followed the sheriff to the door. James thanked him, and Lizzie followed the older man down the path. "What's happening to Damen?"

The sheriff put his hat on his head and looked down at her, frowning. "He's at the station until the MPs com get him, which could be anytime now."

Lizzie thanked him as he sauntered to his cruiser parked out front of their house. Hurricane shutters were being placed up around the neighborhood. The sounds of men working and hammering echoed in the street. Their house was equipped with shutters that were easily closed; James had already shut the rooms they didn't use often. Their gardener would do the rest before the storm came. She felt the urgency of the preparations, the worry that came with the storms, especially one of this predicted strength. Her anxiety rose as she thought about the sheriff's words.

She didn't believe he had anything to do with her sister's disappearance, but it was unsettling with the red words written on the wall. Whoever it was would have been watching for a chance to break in when no one was there. Had they been paying attention to the time she had spent with Damen? A shudder of fear rose in her gut. She needed to see Damen before he left, let him know she didn't believe the accusation. If she hurried, she might make it.

CHAPTER 22

Damen startled at the sudden opening of the inter-view room door. A large man Damen knew as the lo-cal sheriff entered, reaching out to shake his hand. "Well, son, I've sure felt like I was back in the service. Your CO has called to chew me out twice now. You must be an important crew member. You're an active-duty SEAL?"

"Yes, sir." He hoped that this meant he was getting out of here soon. There was not much more of this he could take. They needed to either press charges or let him go.

"I'm informed that you're being escorted out of here shortly by a couple of MPs to hitch a ride back to Norfolk tonight."

This didn't surprise him, sure that his CO was playing a heavy hand in the situation by sending the navy police to escort him. Damen was so ready to leave and get away from this craziness that he'd be willing to go anywhere with the MPs. Although he wanted to say goodbye to Lizzie once more. It wasn't looking good.

The older man handed Damen his phone. "Looks like someone's been trying to reach you. I just left their house."

There were several texts and missed calls from Lizzie. If he'd been by their house, what had he revealed to them? He looked up into the Sherriff's face.

"Don't worry, son. I have a couple of pretty zealous deputies that watch way too much TV. If I need to, and I don't think we will, we'll get a warrant to get fingerprints and DNA. We don't take the word of vandals."

"What did you say to the Legards?" Damen was worried about how Lizzie would react when the sheriff told her he was a suspect in Cami's disappearance, even though it sounded as though he wasn't..

"It's always been my practice, especially in a small town, to let the family know what we found. And I always tell them when we're looking into accusations, enough locals already know what was painted on the walls. It's important to be transparent. Especially for *them*.... There are enough people now knowing what happened during the robbery today. Word's gotten around. It wouldn't be good to let them hear it from anyone else other than me."

"They think I killed their daughter?" Damen asked.

A knock sounded on the door. A clerk stuck her head in. "Sherriff, there's two MPs from the base who want to speak to you."

"Can I leave? I need to get my bags..."

"Sorry, son, there's a crime scene there. Leave us your address and we'll send your things when we're done."

Damen shook his head in disbelief. He'd be out of the country within the next 12 hours, and not coming back for several months. This was a big inconvenience. The sheriff left the room.

He couldn't believe this mess; the day had certainly taken a turn that he didn't expect. Now he was leaving, and the woman he was falling for likely suspected him of murdering her sister. There would be no starting this relationship. It had ended when he dropped her off at her house earlier this afternoon. There was no way that she'd want to stay in touch. They were doomed before they even began.

A heaviness settled in his chest, making it difficult to breathe. He wanted this, but life didn't seem to be ready to let him have it.

The door to the interview room opened slowly, the hinges squeaking. Damen looked up, hopeful to see an MP looking to bring him to base. Instead, Lizzie stuck her head around the door, tentatively looking into the room. Her eyes widening when she saw him, tears brimming. "Damen!" she said, stepping forward, her arms outstretched to embrace him.

Relief filled his cells as he opened his arms to take her in. "Are you all right? I'm so sorry this happened..."

He wrapped her in his arms, laying her face against his chest as he cradled her head in his hands. That she had come to him now spoke volumes. "I'm all right... no worries. Just getting taken through the ringer with questions."

"I heard about the treasure... All that work..."

"Gone, what was there anyway. It wasn't all of it. Some smaller pieces, gold chains, emeralds, some coins.... and your necklace, Lizzie. I'm so sorry." He looked into her face and wiped tears from her cheeks with his thumb. "Don't cry, Lizzie. It's all right..."

"It's so awful. The graffiti ... who would do such a thing?"

Damen's stomach fell. "I hope you know I had nothing to do with..."

She brushed her palm along his cheek. "We don't believe it was you, Damen... *I* don't believe it."

His hopes rose. Not sure he deserved someone as kind as she was. He pulled her into his arms, stroking her hair, relishing the feel in his fingers. Trying to commit it to his memory. "They must have been waiting for us to leave, watching..." she said, pulling back from him to look into his face. "Who could have done such a thing?"

"I don't know."

A knock sounded on the door, and a young man in an MP uniform stepped into the room. "We need to leave, sir, wheels up in 30 minutes."

The short timeline took Damen aback. They had just enough time to make it to the airstrip. Getting across Route 1 was going to be a challenge with all the traffic that would be on the road because of the evacuation order. They needed to leave now. "One minute," he said. The MP stepped from the room.

Damen grasped Lizzie urgently by her upper arms. "This is what I was talking about when I said it's difficult to have a relationship with me. Taking off on short notice and being gone for most of the time is pretty routine. Robberies, accusations and hurricane evacuations aside," he smiled despite himself.

"I'd like to see where this goes," Lizzie answered.

Damen kissed her, his lips meeting hers fully, urgently. The contact immediately flaring that slow burn between them. Underneath the passion, he sensed something more, and that was what he was willing to explore. *If* she really had feelings for him, and wasn't rebounding from Daniel's death, he'd like to know. She'd touched him. He'd not felt like this for anyone, and he wanted to see where it led them.

It was risky. The odds were against them. The distance alone would force them to take it slow, with deployment and her studies. "I'll send you the contact information for when I am overseas. We can video chat," he chuckled, kissing her again.

"I'd like that," she smiled. "I can come down to Norfolk when you get back for a few days."

"It will be the holidays by then. We'll work it out."

She smiled, looking forward to the time she would see him again. Reluctant to leave her, he took her by the hand, and they exited the tiny interview room, joining the MP waiting by the door. He nodded to the uniformed man. "I'm all yours," Damen said, offering both hands to be cuffed. The MP just stared at his hands.

"Sorry sir. We're just here for escort orders from LT- Major Drummond."

"I'm free to go?" Damen asked.

"Yes, sir," the MP answered, following Lizzie and Damen as they exited the building. Several deputies watched their exit, including Paul, a scowl on his face. He wasn't happy Lizzie had come to see him, clearly.

Damen held her hand, trying to get as much contact as he could in the next minutes before he needed to step into the MP's vehicle. He fished in his pocket for his keys. "Could you give these to my father? He'll be looking for them, to put my truck in out of the weather. Just make sure it gets garaged for the hurricane."

"I can't believe all of this is happening so fast. I will get it to him tonight, and if he can't I'm sure there's room in our garage for one more car."

Damen stopped walking in front of an official-looking vehicle. "Here's where I get off." He grabbed Lizzie by her hips, pulling her to him for a deep, passionate kiss. Her lips parted, and he plunged his tongue into her mouth, tasting her, committing the feeling to memory. It would soothe him on those nights that he couldn't sleep, which would be most of them. Life on deployment was rough.

The sound of a throat clearing brought Damen back from Lizzie's mouth. "We need to leave now."

Damen held Lizzie at arm's length, studying her face, trying to make sure the sight was imprinted on his brain. He leaned in for one last brush of lips. "Goodbye Lizzie," he whispered, letting her go and getting into the waiting vehicle.

She raised her fingers to wave at him, tears in her eyes. He turned in the seat as they pulled away, watching as her figure grew smaller in the distance and disappeared completely from view as they turned a corner. He shifted himself in the seat, holding on to the dashboard as the driver expertly maneuvered the jeep through the traffic on their brief trip to the airfield.

All he had on him was his wallet and phone. It would be enough. It had to be. His gear was all on base and he'd stop by his apartment briefly for any personal items if they had time. If not, he'd have to make do with what he stored on base, which was more his home, anyway.

His thoughts were on Lizzie. He wanted to find out if they had a future together, and see if it could really work out. It was not what he ever thought he'd want, but a life ahead with her in it brought a smile to his lips. He hoped they had a chance; he vowed to do what he could to make it possible.

They made it smoothly through the checkpoints, with the MP driving his vehicle right onto the tarmac, where a c-17 cargo plane was being loaded. The transport wasn't fancy, or all that comfortable, but it served its purpose. Damen checked in with the coordinator and boarded the plane, taking a seat near some other enlisted guys. He recognized one man, and they greeted each other. "Going to be a bad one," the younger man said. "I hear already that they are warning those that don't evacuate, that there'll not be anybody coming to help them."

Damen nodded, his mind still on Lizzie. His seatmate kept on talking, unabashed by Damen's non-response. "First time they've evacuated the base, there are some shelters for those that are staying, but the rest of us took the Navy up on a free ride up north."

It didn't seem like this guy would be quiet soon, so Damen leaned back on the bench and closed his eyes, hoping he would take the hint. It worked.

He let his thoughts go back to Lizzie and their afternoon together before the mess with the robbery began. Those memories would be all he had to sustain him for the next several months. He knew it wouldn't be enough. For now, it had to be.

EPILOGUE

Hurricane Irma did billions of dollars in damage to Florida, beginning in the Keys and moving up the west coast of the state where the storm had strengthened over the Gulf after leaving the Keys. It had started out as the most intense hurricane ever to cross the Caribbean, but after hitting Cuba, it lost some of its strength before hitting the Keys. After re-gaining its energy, the storm turned inland and caused damage all the way up the spine of the state after coming ashore in Naples.

Lizzie and her family had fared well after leaving the Keys the day after saying goodbye to Damen outside the police station. Their family house sustained minor roof damage. Isaac Wisler spent the hurricane hunkered down with some friends, where they spent most of it as inebriated as they could be. Salvage work resumed on the *Atocha* a few days after the storm passed through. Life ground into a new normal for everyone.

Marcus struggled once they were back at school. He returned to the Keys, abandoning his education, making no further plans. His depression over losing Daniel wouldn't be shaken. Lizzie did her best to help her cousin but matters in her own world unraveled.

At first, Damen had been in touch every few days. They had several video calls and chats early in his deployment, and things had been going well. Gradually the messages became further and further apart, with Damen withdrawing from her. Eventually, she confronted him, pushing him to communicate his true feelings. It was then Lizzie learned that he'd lost a teammate on a mission that had gone badly. He couldn't share much about the situation because of the classified nature of the work, but it was clear that it had impacted him greatly.

They were in Afghanistan, that much she knew. He was working a lot, taking missions nearly constantly. The situation grew more and more tense in the area as attacks from the Taliban escalated. Watching the news at night, Lizzie could piece together some of what he was likely engaged in, and it terrified her. Losing his co-worker had really impacted him, changing Damen's overall demeanor.

Pushing him brought her an unexpected reaction, making her own heart crumble. "Lizzie, I just can't see putting you through this with me. This is dangerous work, and there is always a chance that I may be injured or killed. Being away like this.... I think we need to re-think ..."

Her stomach had sat in her chest as he spoke, his words cutting into her. She'd lost her best friend, Daniel, and then Marcus had left her and now Damen. In her heart, she knew he was trying to protect her, keep her from having yet another loss in her life. The feelings she had for him had grown even with the distance between them. Love had blossomed in her heart, and he was pulling it away.

"Let's plan on seeing each other over the holidays, like we had planned..."

"And then what, Lizzie? I'm not leaving the service; this has been my life..."

"It's who you are..." she replied, almost whispering, as tears brimmed in her eyes.

"I didn't want it to be like this... I'm sorry Lizzie," he whispered, his fingers touching the screen.

She reached up to lay her hand over his, imagining the connection. Tears glistened in his eyes. Suddenly, their connection became choppy. There was a loud noise, an explosion rocked the barracks. The picture came in and out as the screen froze and restarted several times. In the background, she could see Damen and several other men putting on their helmets and bullet-proof vests. She continued to watch as he approached the computer. He could see his mouth moving to say something, but no sound was coming through the speakers. Her screen went black, the call ended. Her heart beat like a drum in her chest, with concern for his situation. She'd never know now, as their relationship was over.

Over? They'd had a few weeks together, and grew close in her time on the wreck, sharing one glorious afternoon. Had they ended before they'd begun? Her heart grew heavy in her chest, making breathing difficult. In the back of her mind, she knew he was trying to protect her from being hurt any further. But she felt it was her choice to make, not his.

There had been no further communication from him, except for an email sent shortly after their last call. There had been an attempted attack on the base, but they were okay. Lizzie carried the contents of his last email in her purse and read it frequently to remind herself of what they had. He had said he thought he loved her and he loved her enough to release her from waiting for him. He'd explained that he wasn't going to change, he was doing what he loved, but he felt it unfair to ask her to wait for him. If their lives had been different, it would have been possible, but they weren't.

Her heart was broken, and she drifted.

Lizzie kept her promise to Isaac, periodically calling to check in on him. They'd spoken a few times since she'd left for school. The conversations never mentioning Damen, just blow by blows of the progress with the salvage operations. Lizzie was content to just listen to the older man, hoping her calls gave him solace from his grief over Daniel.

Their last call had been different. Isaac had answered the call with his words slurring. It was obvious he'd been drinking and sobbed when he heard her voice. His distress alarmed her, and she couldn't understand what he was saying. Eventually, she got him to calm down so she could understand what had happened, and what he said made her blood run cold. "Oh Lizzie, am I to lose all my children? My boys!.... Damen is missing. There was a helicopter crash on their mission, most of his team were killed. They think he may be dead, and if he's alive... if he's alive.... they'll torture him.... he'll wish he were dead..."

The beeps of the life support machines created an odd symphony over the prone figure laying in the hospital bed. She heard her father's soft voice murmuring down the hallway of the military hospital as he quietly spoke with the attending physician. James had insisted on coming with her once he knew where she was heading.

She couldn't bring herself to step over the threshold. Damen had made clear weeks ago now that he wanted nothing more to do with her. Then why was she here? Guilt? Love?

Damen's head was covered in bandages, and what was visible was not recognizable as the man she once knew. Burns had covered most of one side of his body, and both legs were broken. That he was alive was a miracle. That he survived alone and badly injured in hostile territory for weeks was divine intervention.

She didn't know why she'd come. But she did. She had to see for herself. It wasn't enough for her to have the printed out email confirming their breakup; she needed to see with her own eyes how bad he was, and whether he would survive. Things had changed for them before this, but now she could see that things really had changed for them both.

Damen wouldn't be part of her life, he'd told her so. Before they'd come to the military hospital, she'd known there was a strong chance that he would not recover, and if he did, he would not be the same man that she knew. He'd been unconscious since he had been brought in. The doctor's feared he may not awaken, and if he did, he would be likely to have brain damage or at the very least spinal cord damage. His chances of a full recovery were slim. She could see that now.

Slowly, purposefully, she stepped into his room. Her fingers found his undamaged hand laying on the stark white sheet. She reached out tentatively and laid her hand on his. Tears falling down her face. It wouldn't do for her to stay and act as his girlfriend, holding his hand through his recovery. He hadn't wanted her and wouldn't want that.

James cleared his throat at the door of the room. "Lizzie," he whispered.

She nodded, knowing it was time to go. She bent down and kissed Damen's forehead, covered in bandages. "Forgive me," she whispered quietly so her father wouldn't hear her, and silently she wished him well, saying goodbye.

James took her hand as they walked down the corridor of the quiet hospital. Lizzie felt like a little girl again, holding her father's hand as he made his rounds at the hospital. The hospital had a beautiful garden area for visitors and patients to enjoy while they recovered. She gestured to her father. "Let's find a bench. It looks like a nice place for a conversation."

Lizzie dreaded what she had to tell him. She feared he would be disappointed in her. The world around them fell into a hush as Lizzie and James sat side by side on the serene bench, sheltered by the leafy canopy of a towering tree. A golden beam of sunshine shimmered through the emerald foliage, casting a gentle warmth down upon them.

With a deep inhale, Lizzie reached out and clasped James' hand tightly in hers, alarm crossing his expression. He gazed deeply into her face, as though searching for any hint of what was to come, his calm facade wavering. Lizzie felt the air grow still, as if time had slowed to a halt. She planned her words, knowing how they would affect her father, who had such grand plans for her future. In a voice barely above a whisper, Lizzie spoke, her words heavy with gravity and weight, "Dad, there's been a change in plans."

Lizzie watched the blood drain from her father's face as he awaited the full extent of her revelation, knowing full well this unforeseen shift would forever alter their world and the dreams she'd been pursuing.

NOTE FROM THE AUTHOR

Thank you for reading ***Secrets in the Deep Blue Sea***! I hope you enjoyed it. Please consider leaving a review or a rating on Amazon and/or Goodreads to let other readers know they may also like it. I would really appreciate it! If you'd like to sign up for my newsletter where I share updates to work in progress and freebies or inside deals exclusive to my newsletter list. You can sign up here https://jeuliahesse. com/sign-up-for-newsletter/

Keep reading for a sneak peek at Book 2 in the Deep Blue Sea series, ***Sins in the Deep Blue Sea.***

PREVIEW

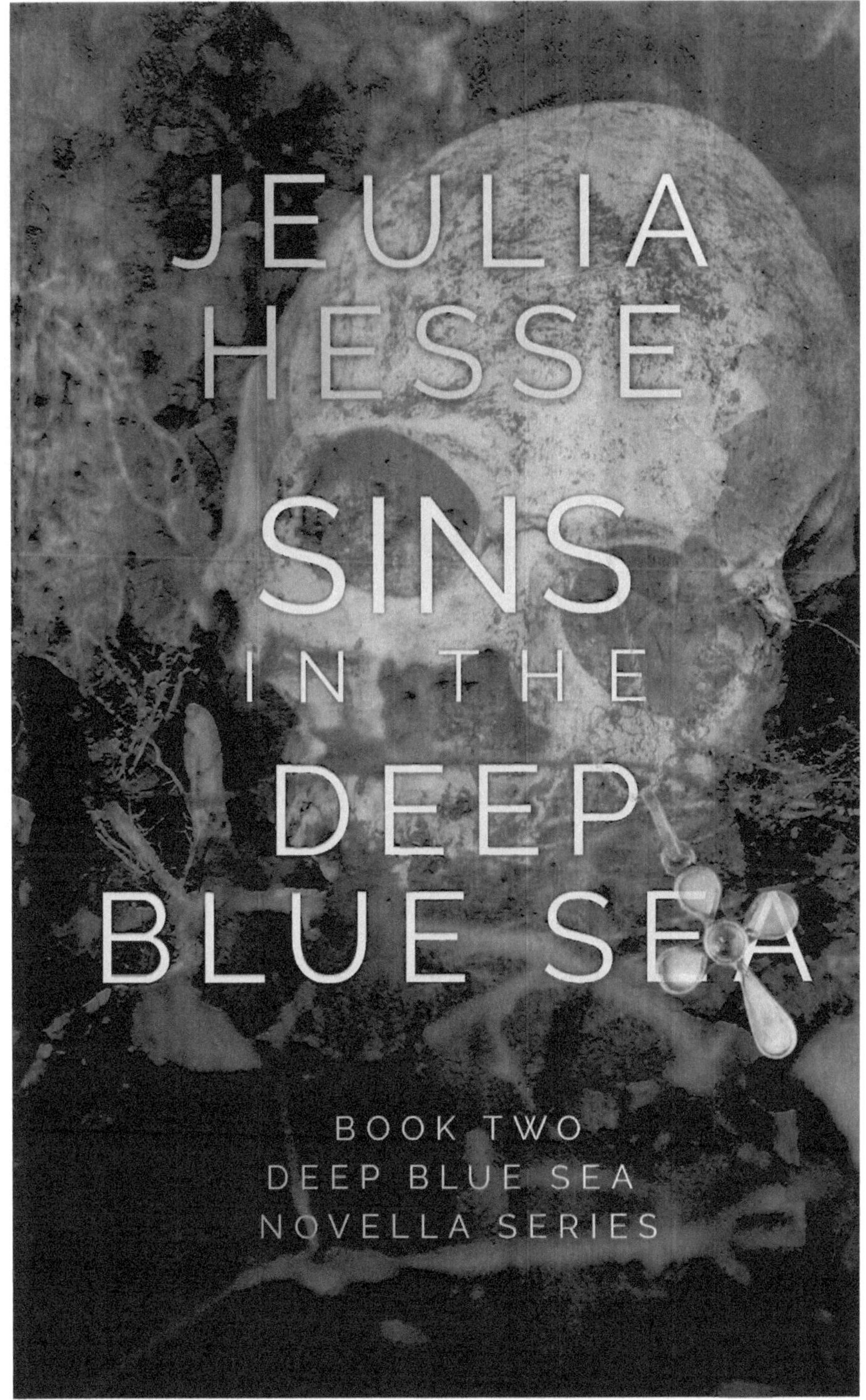
JEULIA
HESSE

SINS
IN THE
DEEP
BLUE SEA

BOOK TWO
DEEP BLUE SEA
NOVELLA SERIES

Chapter 1–2022

The drive down Route 1 through the Keys was beautiful. It was the tail end of the peak tourist season, so the traffic built the further South she drove. The trip from Miami to Key West would take about four hours, time enough to have the space to think. The time to process the information she'd long expected to hear coming thirteen years after her sister had gone missing.

They'd found her remains.

Finally, the mystery of her sister's disappearance was going to end. It was both a great relief and a very sorrowful time. The mixed emotions whirled in Lizzie's stomach, not settling in either place of respite or grief. She wasn't sure how she felt.

She lowered the window, permitting the sea air to fill her lungs. The breeze stirred her from the drowsiness of the solo drive; the air swirling around the staleness of the borrowed car. She'd never planned to come back here. Now gazing at the scenery at the iconic route, it reminded her of her vow to never return.

The place just had too many memories, too much grief. Here she was, the little sister of the girl that had gone missing. A weight she carried throughout most of her life, and not one she wanted to pass down to her own child.

This was where Cami had vanished, where Daniel had drowned and she'd experienced love, only to have her heart shattered. Too many memories that weighed too heavily for her to make it through them all.

Life for her was not here. It was in another tourist town far north of here. Bar Harbor had become her home where her assembled family lived. A group of close friends had grown to be her family. People she shared her life with, not those that were related by blood, but found it difficult to find time for her. It wasn't here.

She had been avoiding thinking or talking about her past in Key West for the last few years. But when Paul Nichols called, she knew she couldn't get away from it any longer. He had been a deputy back then, but now he was the sheriff. It was inspiring how he achieved his ambitions—but unfortunately, his call meant that old secrets were being dragged back up again. Cami's case hadn't made news since they had last spoken—until he reached out just days ago.

They'd found her remains.

But there was more, more that Paul wasn't telling her, except to ask that she come to town. There were circumstances that he didn't want to discuss on the phone that needed to be done face to face. This struck her as very odd, and she called the private investigator that she hired a year ago. Jackson Peters was an ex-ranger who had his own security and private investigation unit. She had found him through a connection with her friend Ashley, the Key West resident psychic Madam Roberta. Ashley had some interesting friends and connections; this one was expensive and very handsome.

Lizzie had a couple of dates with Jackson before employing him to look through her sister's case, but the attempt at a relationship hadn't gone far. She'd had too many commitments in her life, and he was busy with his business. It either wasn't the right time or there was nothing between them. Working together on the case right now seemed to be the most fruitful for both of them.

However, he was the first call she made after hearing from Paul. He'd advised her to see it through, to make the trip and find out what it was he wanted. If there was something substantial, Jackson would come to the Keys and help her sort it out. Lizzie squirmed in her seat. That would be a very expensive sorting out. She hoped it wouldn't come to that; she'd bought a house last year, and funds were tight. Her job as a physician's assistant paid well, but not well enough to afford the fees of Peter's agency to travel there for any extended time. She knew he would cut her a deal because of his friendship with Ashley and his interest in Lizzie. But she didn't want to be beholden to him, or anyone.

The second call she'd made after hearing the news was to her mother. Divorced from her father, Soledad had stayed in Miami after the hurricane evacuated her from her family home, now nearly five years ago. The time had not brought them closer. In fact, they had grown more distant, if that was possible. Her mother was a stranger to her, existing in her extravagant condo overlooking the ocean, continuing to wait for news of her elder child. She was hardly acquainted with her grandchild.

It was her barely used vehicle that she now drove to the Keys after declining a ride on her uncle's private jet. The borrowed car meant one less expense on this trip, and there was not a timeline to return it.

In contrast, Lizzie and her father had grown closer, spending even more time together. So much so that she bought the house next to him. When James moved to Maine, he found a new life, and a new love that Lizzie couldn't help but adore. The warmth between them was so different from the coldness she saw between her parents. It was wonderful having her family so close by. She could depend on them for support when necessary, and they'd frequently get together for backyard barbecues. Very unlike their previous life in the Keys.

Cousin Marcus still lived in the Keys, although they had drifted in their relationship, they still were close. The grief of losing Daniel weighed heavily on Marcus. In recent times, he'd come out to his family and was living his life authentically, no longer in the shadows. He couldn't bring himself to return to school after the semester started up again following Daniel's death. But with his family's wealth, he felt he didn't need to finish his degree. He was staying busy in the booming tourist rental business in the Keys and had a large group of extended friends. Life for him had balanced out.

Lizzie had kept in touch, though minimally, with Isaac Wisler. She knew she would need to stop in to see him at the assisted living where he now lived. Isaac became very sick because of heavy smoking and drinking, and the sadness of losing his son Daniel and Damen's accident. The treasure from the *Atocha* had been mostly recovered.

Isaac had gained wealth and recognition from the discovery and artifacts, but it had not been enough to make up for the loss that his family had suffered. Lizzie knew she needed to pay him a visit to ease her sense of guilt, although he would surely find out she was in town, anyway. She didn't want to disappoint him further.

What she wanted during this trip was to avoid seeing Damen. After his helicopter crash, he'd been found miraculously alive after several weeks of evading the Taliban. It was amazing he hadn't succumbed to his injuries while also avoiding capture. Sheer will must have kept him alive. In the weeks he'd been missing, everyone had thought him dead, including her.

She shook off the old fear and anxiety that rose whenever she remembered that time in her life. He ended their relationship before the crash because he didn't want her to worry about him while he fought terror around the world. He wanted her to move on with her life and be a doctor, as her father had planned.

Somewhere in her jewelry box, she'd kept the last email he wrote to her, the final breaking off of their relationship. Occasionally, she read it to herself whenever she needed a reminder of her choices and her life's path from then to now.

After staying in the hospital for a while and going through a long period of recovery, they released Damen from the Navy. Because of the severity of his injuries, he could no longer serve as a SEAL operator.

The last she knew from Marcus was that he'd returned to the Keys to run his father's salvage company and had been branching into other business ventures. He had been the one to provide her with the details of his condition, even when she didn't ask. After a lengthy recovery and rehabilitation, Marcus reported Damen had lost the function in one eye. And had some other non-visible injuries, apart from a slight unevenness in his stride. Marcus had remarked about his visible scars, making him appear more the beast that little brother Daniel always referred his older brother as. Apparently, he'd become quite the successful, even though the business now rarely searched for a new treasure, and when it did, Damen did not join them.

If he was in town, she'd like to avoid seeing him at all. In her mind, there was no reason to dredge up their brief time together, no need to connect. He'd made his choice when he ended their relationship, making it abundantly clear he wanted no part of her in his life. Lizzie had made her choice as well, years ago.

There would be no going back.

About the Author

Jeulia Hesse is an emerging author of mystery, suspense, and romance fiction. She hails from sunny Florida where she lives with her husband spending the winter months escaping the snow and cold of her native Vermont, where the author summers among family and friends.

If you would like book release updates and exclusive give-aways/contests, please subscribe to her newsletter at www.jeuliahesse.com